Christmas Affair

Book Two of the Stonewater Stories
By
Ginny Frost

Copyright

This is a work of fiction. Names, characters, places, and incidents are either the product of the author's imagination or are used fictitiously, and any resemblance to actual persons living or dead, business establishments, events, or locales, is entirely coincidental.

Christmas Affair

Contact Information: ginnyfrost@ginnyfrost.com

Ginny Frost

PO Box 4686

Halfmoon, NY 12065-9211

Visit me at www.ginnyfrost.com

Published in the United States of America

Edited by Sandra Nguyen of Untangled Yarns: Fiction and Nonfiction

Cover Image via depositphotos.com by prostooleh

Dedication

For Robbie and Tobi
    And all that sibling stuff

Acknowledgements

A huge thank you to both Grace and Jenna for their help in my research about Celiac disease. Nothing like getting data from people who've had to deal with the real thing. Thank you.

Thank you to my editor, Sandra, for working so quickly and efficiently to help me get the book ready in time.

Thank you to my beta readers: Kari, Lisa, and Jen. You all made the story so much better.

Chapter One

Josephine Lockwood placed her computer bag by the reception desk of the Excelsior Hotel. The rest of her luggage sat piled at the curb with a struggling bellboy. The bizarre gothic-deco design of the hotel baffled her. But Mom insisted the Excelsior was the place to be in Iverton.

Whatever.

Jo could endure a weekend full of winter sports and a large Christmas party Saturday night. It was the same every year, but this time Mom insisted she bring a week's worth of clothes.

Why?

It didn't matter. Her computer bag with all its tiny devices tucked around her laptop contained everything she needed.

The machine was her life, and Mom didn't have a clue. Jo wondered if customized makeup bags were available to hide all her techno goodies. Then she wouldn't have to explain about the computer bag every single time she slung it over her shoulder.

A project for another day.

This weekend epitomized downtime. Jo wanted nothing more than to curl up in front of a roaring fire while the rest of the party skied, skated, and celebrated the holidays.

Mom refused to allow Jo to participate in outdoor activities. According to Mom, the Upstate New York cold would be too much for her lungs. Sometimes Jo protested, but since she hated skiing anyway... She'd tried it once, behind Mom's back. It was cold, and awkward, and she fell off the chairlift. She'd sworn off the sport forever.

Since she detested winter sports, a large fireplace with a cup of cocoa constituted the perfect setting for fixing last-minute tweaks in her sample program. And Mom would let her sit and surf if she thought Jo was perusing dating sites.

At the front desk, the two young ladies working hardly noticed her. They twittered to each other, their gaze caught by something off to the side. Jo leaned over the counter to see the distraction. Her breath caught in her throat before she composed herself.

The human equivalent of a Norse god stood speaking with a man of color in a suit in the office. The earthbound deity wore a simple t-shirt and jeans with a tool belt across his hips like a gunslinger. Jo's skin tingled at the sight of him—all blonde, tall, and muscular. His crossed arms highlighted his muscular biceps and triceps. Even his forearms said he worked out every day, all day.

The other man barely hit her radar, though he was well-dressed and sharply handsome. But between the two of them, no wonder the women were distracted. Jo cleared her throat, hoping to rip their gaze away from the men.

A loud snicker caught the men's attention. They both eyed the desk.

The girls blushed as if they'd been staring at the sun too long. One, whose nametag read Tiffany, finally noticed Jo waiting. She scanned Jo up and down, her nose wrinkling slightly, the air heavy with disdain.

"I'm so sorry. How can I help you?" Her grin looked painted on. Jo wished people could just be themselves.

"Good afternoon," she answered, smiling. "I'm Josephine Lockwood." As soon as her name dropped, the girls' demeanor changed. Judgy and condescending morphed into polite and butt-kissing.

"Oh, Ms. Lockwood. You're here!" Tiffany practically squeed.

The other clerk, Arabella by her nametag, hopped up and down. "We're so glad you've finally arrived."

Finally here? Jo was early, but... Mom must have sent her demands ahead for the "special care" Jo required. She sighed, hating the fuss. But she was used to it.

Mom always made a huge deal about Jo, never letting her lift a finger for anything. Hell, carrying in her own computer bag today felt like a treat. Usually, someone snatched whatever she carried out of her hands before she knew what was happening.

"Everything is set. We're all so excited. It's going to be a fantastic visit," Arabella said. Tiffany gave the girl a hard look and a harder elbow to the ribs. The two women exchanged glances and Arabella added, "For the Christmas party." She raised her hands above her head in triumph. "Just don't use the escalator."

Jo stared at her quizzically. Mom's party was a bigger deal than she thought—either that or Arabella must be starved for fun.

"Uh, sounds good." Jo glanced behind her as the bellboy puffed in with a cart full of her luggage. "I'd like to check in now."

Tiffany's plastic grin grew wider. She spoke, hardly moving her lips. "Great. We have you in the Presidential Suite. Here are your keys. Zed will accompany you upstairs. Please call the desk if you need anything." She cocked her head toward the elevator, her smile as fake as ever.

"Don't you want my ID or credit card, or..."

Arabella cut her off. "It's already taken care of, Ms. Lockwood. Enjoy your stay."

Mom, of course.

With an eyeroll, Jo headed to the indicated hallway, the bellboy close behind. As the doors closed, a burst of laughter escaped the girls again. A conversation in high-pitched squeals followed.

Jo looked at Zed, who shrugged.

"They're overexcited about everything. They aren't supposed to work the same shift anymore, but we've got all hands on deck for the weekend. Plus the renovations." He passed a shy grin Jo's way before exiting the car onto her floor.

The tension in the air hinted that many more activities were in store besides Mom's Christmas party. She'd have to look up the hotel events.

The hope of something more interesting than dry chicken and septuagenarians stirred her heart. Something new, something exciting, something out of the ordinary—an adventure.

Or if she hid in her room, she could skip the entire affair.

That sounded like heaven.

Brett Kramer raised his eyebrows at the ruckus emanating from the front desk. The Excelsior was a classy place, not usually filled with the giggling cadence of young women losing their minds. The two girls at the desk had been eye-fucking him since he entered the office. He shook his head, done with immature women.

His gaze returned to Stanley, who sat on the edge of a desk in the sizeable office space.

"You were saying..." Stanley pursed his lips, seeming to hide a grin.

Brett narrowed his eyes at Stanley's sarcasm. "Why do you put those two tweens out on the desk together? Geez, what a racket. Do they give you the 'come-hither' look, too?"

The manager grinned. "They're new. I rarely have them on together, but we have a couple events this week. I booked every room not under construction. So, if you finish the west wing, I can fill the space. Hint hint."

Brett shook his head. "Sure, if your guests won't mind sharing the can with the room next door. The tiling is almost done. I have four of the seven new toilets installed. The last three are in those creepy little rooms in the back. Do you rent those?"

The job at the Excelsior was a godsend. Kramer and Sons Contracting of Stonewater always had a great run from spring through fall. But come winter, the work dried up. He and his family were used to the ebb and wane of the business, but this year had been tight. They'd gotten fired from a job last winter. For the rest of the year, people seemed a little leery to hire them—well, townies anyway, not the summer people.

Stonewater was a great town, but not big enough to support all the carpenters. Dad's marketing plan comprised nothing but word of mouth. The business never expanded beyond himself, Dad, and Ted. Not to mention, they'd missed the bid on the new kitchen in the Greenview Inn a while back. It didn't look great when the biggest makeover in town went elsewhere. Hell, even little brother Ryan had left for larger fields.

Now that Dad was older, Brett planned to take over the business and turn it into a real money maker. He'd hire more guys with him and Ted supervising bigger jobs. They'd run real advertising, not a note in the local paper. A string of jobs at ski lodges meant steady work year-round.

But Brett and Stanley Frasier, the current manager at the Excelsior in Iverton, were tight from way back. When the renovation deal came up at the hotel, Stan arranged the subcontract with Drake Incorporated. Brett snagged the contract before the words died on Stanley's lips.

The work moved quickly when Ted helped. With only sinks, toilets, and a few tiles left to install, Ted returned home to help with a local job. Brett stayed to finish and grab a few more trips down the slopes for free—another great perk.

Hell, if Spencer Drake liked the result, he might hire the Kramers for more jobs. Most of the time, only Ted and Brett worked, and Mr. Drake hedged at contracting them for a larger project. They'd compromised with renovating one of the older sections. The rooms were pure seventies with avocado tubs and orange wallpaper.

Stanley broke into his thoughts. "If you'd hurry and finish, I could rent those units. Call them econo-rooms and charge a little less." He grinned, ever the salesman. "How much longer?"

Brett shrugged, hooking his thumbs in his tool belt. "Not more than two days. By Sunday, for sure. But I bet I can wrap by Saturday afternoon." The two men exchanged a fist bump in agreement.

"Good, then I'll steal your room for Saturday night. There's a crazy wedding asking for more and more rooms. Don't they realize it's the holiday season? I told the woman we were booked, but she doesn't like 'no' for an answer. I'm not bumping paying guests for her people. They can stay at the Charles or Greenview in Stonewater. Decent places, but not the Excelsior." Stanley winked.

One of the desk-twins stuck her head in the office. "Mr. Frasier?" Stanley lifted his chin in acknowledgment. "A guest needs help in the Presidential Suite. Something about a stuck door."

Stanley waved her off. "Call Ernie. He's on for the weekend."

"I did." She paused for a moment to flutter her eyelashes at Brett, who looked at her blankly.

Jailbait had no place on his menu.

"He's dealing with the escalator... again." She put a finger to her lips, letting the edge of the nail slip inside. "Can he go?"

Slowly, she removed her finger to point at Brett.

He assumed the act was supposed to be erotic, but his gut churned. He glanced at Stanley, who shrugged.

"Unless you're pressed, can you handle this? I'll throw more hours on your timecard."

Brett shrugged. "Sure, no problem. Stuck door?" The clerk nodded. "Got it." He headed toward the exit, but the girl didn't move out of his way. She stared at him, starry-eyed, her bottom lip caught in her teeth. With a smile, he put one hand on each of her shoulders and rotated her to the side so he could pass.

Women.

He was done with immature twenty-somethings chasing him down. He had plenty of luck in the lady department, but lately, everyone pursuing him fell way out of his age range. Where were the women in their early thirties with an education, a job, and no kids? Nonplussed, he headed to the elevators. "What room?" he called without looking over his shoulder.

"The Presidential Suite," one girl called with a snigger.

As he entered the car, the girl added, "I bet she'll think he's a stripper." A tumult of giggles erupted from the desk area.

"Wait. What?" Brett asked as the door shut.

Chapter Two

Upstairs, Brett knocked on the Presidential Suite's door. No answer. He rattled the handle. He waited a beat and knocked again. No answer. With Stanley's passkey, Brett opened the door a crack.

"Hello?" he called.

Silence.

Maybe the patron was stuck behind a door inside the room.

Crap.

He didn't want to walk into a bizarre situation. The word "stripper" echoed in his head.

Please God, don't let me step into a bachelorette party.

He did not sign up for that. Checking the nameplate on the door again—*yep, the Presidential Suite*—he stepped into the room.

A few suitcases stood stacked by the closet. The seating area by the television looked fresh and untouched. Through the doorway, he could see the bedroom, the bed made, everything pristine.

"Hello?" he called again. "Maintenance." It worked for the maids.

"Thank God," a muffled voice sounded from somewhere in the huge space. "Please hurry."

"Uh, sure. Be right there." He moved further inside, still not spotting the resident. "Where are you?"

"I'm out here," came the muted reply.

He headed for the bedroom, praying there weren't a dozen drunk and horny women behind the bed. He found no one lurking inside the lavish and elegant space. Relief rushed over him.

The bathroom door stood open, so no one was locked in there. He scratched his head as he rotated in a circle when a booming knock caught him off guard. He finally saw her.

A pale face peeked through the break in the curtain covering the windows of the balcony. *She's outside?*

Brett hurried over and scooted the curtain aside. A young woman stood on the room's tiny balcony, wearing nothing but a silk bathrobe. Anxiety and anger marred her pretty face. Her lips looked blue. In one hand, she held a cell phone.

Ah, that's how she contacted the desk.

Instead of a slider, the balcony had a large glass door that opened into the room. Good. Hinges on the inside helped.

His gaze slid over the little brunette in the robe. He'd seen a glimpse of her in the lobby but had not registered how adorable she was. Her round face was delicate. Her skin looked porcelain. Everything about her seemed elfin, fine, rich, and breakable. Would a girl like that last a round with a man like him, tall and hung? Half a grin formed on his lips.

As he studied the door, she knocked again. "I'm freezing here."

Brett snapped back to reality.

Door. Fix. Now.

He tried the handle. The thing came off in his hand. On the other side, the young woman held up the other half.

Well, crap. But fixable.

Brett knelt and examined the mechanism. With a screwdriver from his belt, he removed the plate over the lock. Still using the same tool, he threaded it through the spindle hole left by the missing handles. Carefully, he drew the latch back.

"Push it open."

Brett scooted back to give the door room to swing. When he moved, the screwdriver slipped just as she smacked the glass.

"Seriously? My toes are falling off!" She appeared rather icy, and not just by her expression.

"Hold on. It slipped."

"It slipped?" she asked, incredulous.

He said nothing as he pressed the latch again with the tool. "Push."

This time the door swung in. She squeezed through the opening and dashed into the suite, exclaiming the entire way, "Oh my God. Oh my God. Oh my God."

Brett refrained from watching her run in the little silk robe. The poor woman looked half frozen. *Warming her could be fun.* Eyes closed, he shut his brain down. Sex while on a job had ruined more than one contract.

Jo scrambled into the bedroom, every inch of her pure ice. She grabbed the spread off the bed and wrapped it around herself. What had she been thinking, going out on the balcony? Yes—the beautiful view of the cliff side, frozen waterfalls, and the ice-covered pines. And then the door shut. No biggie until the handle came off in her hand. Thank God, the maintenance guy had been close by, though he took his time getting the thing open.

Her body trembling like an earthquake, she flipped the bedspread over her head into a hood. Only the tip of her nose and her feet stuck out. She tiptoed to the seating area, her legs refusing to move quickly. The Norse god of a maintenance man fiddled with the still-open balcony door.

"Please, can you close the door?" she asked, looking around the room for the thermostat. "It's freezing out there."

"Yes, ma'am," he said with the usual upstate inflection she'd heard many times on these trips north. "But I gotta put the handle and the plate back on." He didn't turn to glance at her.

"I don't plan on going out there ever again. Lucky, I brought my cell with me and could call for help."

Still facing the door, he shrugged. "Handles break. But if I leave it, you'll have a hole in the wall. Not great for keeping the heat in."

This time, he turned and gave her the full brunt of his gaze. Bright gray-brown eyes twinkled at her. "We gotta warm you up, right?" His voice sounded all charm, and it added heat to her skin.

With a narrowed gaze, she assessed him.

Rugged, rural New Yorker type, handy and handsome. He probably spent as much time repairing things as he did "servicing" his clients. She'd bet half the hotel patrons dallied with the hottie. Oh well. At least, he saved her and fixed the lock.

"Well... Please hurry," she said. How did her mother find it so easy to order people around? Jo only did it when she felt mad, and mad passed through her easily. Now she was merely frozen and embarrassed. Trembling with cold, she pulled a hand from the covers to adjust the thermostat. Her fingers shook so badly, she hit every button twice. After five resets, she sputtered in frustration.

"Here, let me." His voice was a deep rumble. "It's gonna take a bit for the room to heat. Go into a smaller room like the bathroom." It made sense. "Actually," he continued, scrubbing his chin after he'd set the temperature to eighty, "let's put you in the tub."

Turning, she tried to huff at him, but the coverlet betrayed her. Wrapped so tightly, she couldn't maneuver, and she toppled. The man caught her before she hit the floor.

"I can feel the cold through the blanket. The tub is best to avoid hypothermia."

She repressed the urge to protest as he hefted her in his arms and carried her to the bathroom. For a rescue, it wasn't half bad. Part of her wanted him to stop in the bedroom and warm up the old-fashioned way. She kept her lips tightly sealed. Well, metaphorically. Her teeth chattered.

"You know so much about the cold."

"Upstate born and bred, my dear. It's cold here most of the year. Gotta keep yourself warm skiing, ice fishing, and the like."

He deposited her on the vanity chair in the bathroom. "Give me a sec here." He bent over—a marvelous view—and drew on the taps. Dual faucets poured water into the giant tub. After a few seconds, steam rose from the water.

"Stanley upgraded the water heaters. Good thing, too." He ran his fingers under the flow and readjusted the knobs. "Be right back. The tub'll fill in a minute." He stood, flashed her a quick grin, and exited the bathroom.

The warm water beckoned her. Loosening the blanket, Jo leaned over toward the tub. She let her fingers dance under the tap.

Heaven.

Tingles danced up and down her hand as the feeling returned. She sank onto the floor, placing both hands in the hot water, savoring the warmth on her skin.

Oh, screw it.

She nudged the bedspread off her shoulders and climbed into the tub. The water barely rose above a few inches, but the heat seeped into her body. She moaned in joy as the cold slowly faded.

"I guess that's one way to do it." The maintenance man stood in the bathroom door, a steaming mug in his hand. "You probably shoulda taken the robe off, if you didn't want to ruin it."

Jo glanced down, noticing her beautiful purple silk was drenched, and didn't care. She held up her hands for the mug, "For me? Thank you so much." She found her manners and gave him a smile.

Kneeling by the tub, he handed her the cup—tea, by the smell. "You sure you're okay? I can call for a first aid kit, maybe get a doctor in here..." He trailed off, turning his head away.

Jo realized her wet robe clung to every inch of her. She slid down, wishing for bubbles. "I think the bath and the tea will help," she said, feeling a fool.

"Uh, okay." He stood and tugged at the towels on the racks. "For when you get out. I guess I'll go." When he ducked out the door, the manly maintenance man's cheeks shone red.

"Wait!" she called, remembering more of her manners. He leaned his head around the doorway. His gaze dipped down for a millisecond before meeting her eyes. "You rescued me, and I don't know your name."

The pink rose higher in his cheeks, almost to his hairline. "Brett Kramer, ma'am." He tipped an invisible cap and disappeared.

Chapter Three

What the hell was that?

Brett closed the door, his heart racing. The sight of the woman in the tub with a purple robe floating around her was permanently etched in his mind. He blinked, trying to dismiss the image, but it refused to fade. Ninety percent of his brain and one hundred percent of his body said, "Go get her." But his last bit of reason stated loudly, "The handyman and the hot chick in a hotel room. Porn movie much?"

And she was not the adult movie type. She seemed classy. Taking advantage of her in her vulnerable state would be wrong. And she appeared, well, delicate. Either the alabaster skin or the fine features made him want to cover her in bubble wrap, not take her over the arm of the couch.

Shaken, he stepped out of the elevator where a chorus of giggles greeted him. The two desk clerks whispered and pointed as he strode by, headed for the older section of the building. He didn't acknowledge them as he passed. *Why are women always so difficult? Why can't I find a tough, self-assured girl who likes power tools?*

When he came to the office, Stan stuck his head out. "Any problems?" His smirk seemed extra obnoxious. What was the deal with the woman in the Presidential Suite?

"Handle fell off her balcony door, locked outside. You might want your regular guy to check those. Luckily, she had her cell." Brett tried to march on, but Stanley asked another question.

"And that's it?"

Brett turned and gave his friend a hard stare. "Yeah, butthead. That's it. I fixed the door. Call her room in ten minutes and make sure she doesn't have hypothermia."

Stanley's eyes opened wide, and he seemed taken aback. "Oh, yeah—uh, sure. Thanks for fixing that, Brett."

Today was weird. But it didn't matter. With only a couple more bathrooms to finish, he could enjoy the nightlife at the hotel's bar. He'd stretch out the last bits of the job till Sunday. Maybe the woman in the Presidential Suite would be at the bar...

Humming, Brett headed back to work.

Jo loved her suite, despite her ordeal with the balcony and the interaction with the maintenance man. Her mother and the rest of the party planned on arriving that evening and the following morning. Tonight, she could sit in the lounge, work on the laptop, and enjoy the view by the fire.

All those years of bed rest took a toll on a girl. Jo came alive when she found the online world of internet forums, webcomics, and gaming sites—especially the programming forums. She'd learned to write code in a dozen languages, old and new. Online, she was Jo-reg (her screen name) instead of Josephine Lockwood, invalid. She liked Jo-reg so much better.

Jo-reg didn't have a mother who always fussed over her, never letting her do for herself. She'd been healthy for a while, but her mother never noticed. Jo learned how to live with the disease diagnosed a year ago. No more asthma or breathing issues. No more constant colds or rashes. In her own controlled environment, she kept the place free of allergens, including her food.

Her mom still coddled her like a baby. But with her sample game almost finished, this was Mom's last weekend, her last hold over Jo's life. After she attended Mom's over-the-top holiday party, Jo was free to start her career and so much more.

Scary, but exciting.

Once outside the elevator, she headed to the large lounge in the back of the hotel. A wall of windows gave an amazing view of the cliff side, snow-covered and winter perfect. The room was oversized, but the hotel cut the space into cozy nooks and crannies with large couches and chairs. A discreet bar huddled in one corner, and tables spotted the area—a ski lodge feel, but warmer, richer, cozier.

Two immense fireplaces glowed with heat at either end, with sad attempts at holiday decorations on the mantle. *Boy, this place could use a woman's touch*. The enormous hearths could each fit an entire dining room table inside them. Their size, with the huge roaring fires, both intimidated and invited one into the space. The two eight-foot pines in the center, decorated with white, gold, and red, threw a better air of Christmas throughout the room. Combined with the bank of windows looking out on a winterscape, the room dispelled the gloomy atmosphere of the rest of the hotel.

She had an hour or two before she needed to play hostess tonight. The fireside called to her, a perfect place to work on her sample project. She was layered up in a turtleneck, wool sweater, and winter-weight pants, but after the balcony fiasco, she remained a little cold.

The perfect little table sat off to one side. She hooked up her laptop and opened her game. Her sample program for Ezgamez was almost perfect. She'd scouted for weeks to find the right company with a wide audience. She'd had offers from others, but Ezgamez matched her "dream job" checklist nearly point for point.

Her program was simple—a three-match game with a simple story. She'd spent hundreds of hours polishing it and adding bonus material to make it shine. She'd probably gone over the top, but Ezgamez's large platform pushed her to excel with her audition piece. She wanted this job more than anything.

The program still needed a few more tweaks. Being alone in the lounge tonight would give her "mom-free" time to finish. If the game passed the test, and she got a job offer, she'd get her own place. She'd live alone without Mom hovering over her every move.

She'd be free.

She'd been hunching over her laptop for about a half an hour when her stomach growled ominously. Not surprising as her trek into the cold probably burned two days' worth of calories. She was careful about what she ate, worried wheat-filled food would trigger a stomach issue. But right now, she could eat an entire stockyard.

Time to snag a roaming server for a snack. Or to pack up and hit the dining room proper.

A quick survey of the room said no one from her mother's party arrived yet, but a tall man stood at the bar—the maintenance guy, Brett Kramer.

She thought she should apologize for being weird and not thanking him properly. And he was awfully cute. *So... Ask him to dinner?*

Ignoring the code scrolling across her page, she bit her lip. *Why not?* He was kind and didn't ogle her, though she'd been half naked. He even blushed. *Time to be bold.*

With pure bravado, she packed her laptop and strolled over to the bar. After a deep breath, she stuck her hand out in front of Brett. "Hi. Remember me? The Presidential Suite? I'm Jo."

He turned to face her, his gray-brown eyes flashing. "I remember something about the Presidential Suite. Door handle, right?" He winked, and the relief flooded over her. He wasn't a dick and didn't joke about her being stupid or naked.

Phew.

"Yeah, thank you for that. I regret..." She waved a hand, unsure how to finish the sentence.

"That you probably had a touch of hypothermia, and I shouldn't have left you alone in a full bathtub. Yes, please apologize." He smirked lightheartedly. But pink crept up his neck again.

So adorable.

"I'm sorry, Jo. I should have stayed and made sure you were okay. Or called the manager or something. You're okay, right?"

She smiled, ducking her head. Heat burned on her own face. "I was fine, just cold. And feeling stupid and embarrassed. Who goes out on a balcony in a bathrobe?"

Brett leaned an elbow on the bar, his gaze square with hers. "Someone who thinks a high-class place like this won't have broken doors. I did go to the manager and report it. It took me a minute to stop being a dick, but Stanley told me he'd check on you."

"Yes, I got a call from the desk from a giggling little girl. She made a snide joke. 'Did I enjoy the maintenance man?' What's with that?"

Brett shook his head, looking dumbfounded.

"Anyway, I asked for the manager. Told him I was fine, you did a great job, and that his registration clerk made sexual innuendos at me." She chuckled, not her usual play, but Mom paid lots of money for the weekend. The staff could at least be polite.

"Damn," Brett said, holding up a beer. "Well done. Can I buy you a drink to say sorry for walking out? You were in the tub, and I—"

Jo waved off his platitudes. "Let me buy you dinner to say sorry for being weird."

He glanced away, and Jo thought for sure he'd decline. *So much for being assertive and trying new things.* She pressed her lips, sorry she didn't accept his drink offer right away. Mom's friends would be here soon, and she'd eat with them if she had to. And of course, her stomach chose that moment to growl.

"Well," he said with a laugh, "how could I turn you down after that?"

Jo slapped her forehead. "And the embarrassment continues..." She sighed. "Thanks anyway, Brett. It was nice to meet you."

He brushed his fingers on her arm as she turned away. "So, no dinner?" he asked sincerely.

"Oh." Now her face positively blazed. "Dinner sounds great. All that cold..."

He laughed, holding his arm out in an invitation to the dining room. "After you, Jo."

A dinner invite? What a surprise. Especially after he'd torn out of her room. She was naked, kinda, and he was no doctor. His thoughts were still muddled after the encounter with the clerk again. Luckily, he came back to his right head.

And Jo apologized to him.

What a world.

When he entered the lounge, he'd spotted her typing on a laptop. He'd planned to go over to her table and make an excuse after he'd finished his beer.

But surprise, surprise. She'd come over, apologized, and invited him to dinner. Anyone coulda knocked him over with a feather.

Warm once again, her skin took on a lovely pink hue. Her brown hair was piled on top of her head, and she wore a sweater that looked like pure comfort. Casual, smiley, and nice. He'd treat her to a meal and snag the best seat in the house too.

He and Jo walked to the formal dining room. The oddly tiered room resembled comedy club seating, but instead of a stage, the space faced the fountain below the elevators of the new wing.

She glanced at her clothes. "I might not be dressed for..." She spotted at his flannel shirt and jeans and stopped talking.

"I've got an in." He leaned over and whispered to the *maître d',* who waved for them to follow.

"Oh, I don't want to impose or anything." She blushed. *Cute.* Hopefully, she wasn't part of the overbearing holiday party here for the weekend. She'd booked the suite, but she seemed nice.

"No imposition. It's how I do dinner most nights. The kitchen staff is awesome."

Jo must have noticed they were heading for the staff doors. She tugged at his arm. "Brett, I don't want to..."

"Trust me."

The *maître d'* held open the swinging door. "This way, *s'il vous plaît.*" He bowed, allowing them to pass.

Jo's fingers tightened. "In the kitchen?" she hissed in a whisper.

"Best seat in the house."

Chapter Four

Jo stood wide-eyed, watching the bustle of the busy space. Stainless steel covered every surface, and dozens of people worked at a clipped pace. The aromas floating in the room grabbed her attention and drew her up short. Inhaling a deep breath through her nose, she fell against Brett's chest, woozy with delight.

He put his hand on her shoulder. The warmth seeped through to her bones, and she repressed a shiver. "You okay there, tiger?" His voice was light and humming, as if giddy with the delicious smells, too. "Our spot is right there."

He steered her to a small table, adorned with holly and a white rose, and away from the busy lanes of traffic.

Brett pulled her seat out. Almost robotic, she sat, her fantasies on hold. How was it any different from dinners with her mother? Coddled, pampered, and put in a corner. She wanted to retreat from the porcelain-doll treatment. Mom gave her enough of that already. She sat stiffly and failed to meet his gaze.

"Okay, it's weird, right? But I hope this fancy 'eat in the kitchen' thing like on TV might be a treat." He dropped in his chair, grabbed a napkin, and shook it out. "They don't let patrons do it here. It's the only place I'm allowed to eat, being the hired help and all. But it's still fun. Gerard, the *maître d'*, plans to work on the new owners to make it an actual thing for paying customers. I hope you don't mind being a guinea pig."

Jo blinked at him, startled. She pulled back from the table, ready to go. *What was that supposed to mean?* She'd made a terrible mistake inviting him to dinner. This would not be the intimate setting she imagined. "I don't know..." She stood.

Brett jumped from his seat. "Oh, man. Sorry about my crappy manners. Is it okay? Eating with the help? I mean, you asked me, but Stanley doesn't want us guys"—he gestured to the kitchen crew—"eating in the big room. I'll grab something to go, and we can eat in the lounge." He said the words in a rush but didn't seem embarrassed or chagrinned. Just genuinely worried about her mental state. The condescending undertone Jo usually heard from her mother was absent.

Cocking her head, she studied him. Perhaps she saw things that weren't there. He did pull her inside after a near-icicle episode. Maybe he was a caring person and not putting her on a pedestal. She bit her bottom lip, considering.

"Okay, no answer. I'll talk to the chef, and if you still want to eat with me, I'll meet you in the lounge." Disappointment peppered his tone.

His lack of fret spoke to her. None of her "mother hen" senses sparked. "No, I'm sorry. I... uh... I have a strict diet."

He looked her up and down. "You don't need to diet. You look great. And the food here is pretty good." His statement roused a cheer among the kitchen staff. Brett grinned over at them. He was funny, too. *Nice.*

"No, I mean, I have to be careful what I eat. Allergies." She slipped back into her seat, hoping she'd made up for her assumptions, hoping Brett might still join her... Hoping he'd see beyond her glass exterior.

"Oh yeah? My dad is allergic to eggs and most nuts. We had an interesting childhood. My brothers and I binged on baked goods when Dad was away. Then we'd hide the evidence when he got back."

Jo's shoulders fell as the embarrassment of her food issues dropped away. He understood that not everyone could eat everything.

"So, what's your poison?" He laughed. "That's a loaded statement. They limit our choices, but if you tell the cook about your allergies, they'll work around it." Brett waved one guy over. The man grabbed a note pad and stood poised and ready to write the order.

She ducked her head, hating to say the words that everyone overreacted to. "Okay, I need gluten-free, please." She said them without meeting the eye of either the server or Brett. Bracing herself, she readied for the onslaught of nonsense advice that came next.

She'd only had the celiac diagnosis for a short time and remained self-conscious about telling people. Learning about her disease had been pure luck.

Her massage therapist caught it. Jo had never paid attention to the trending diets, gluten-free, paleo, and whatnot. But once, during a session, her masseuse, Grace, noticed a rough patch on her back.

"Looks like one of those gluten rashes," she'd said, holding up a mirror. Clumps of little red dots dotted Jo's back. "I had another client with this. She went gluten-free, and her skin has been clear ever since."

The next day, Jo demanded tests from her GP for celiac disease. Since then, her life opened up. She felt so much better, her skin became flawless, and the migraines disappeared. Best of all, she'd started thinking about a real future and sent her resume to Ezgamez.

But the universe didn't always understand she had an allergy.

Back in the kitchen, shoulders hunched, Jo waited for Brett's armchair-doctor impression. It never arrived.

Brett said nothing.

The server smiled. "We have a large selection. Are you here for the big party? We have a ton of gluten-free options for it."

Jo let out a breath. Mom had listened for once. Perhaps sending the medical report opened her eyes. Once a doctor gave a diagnosis, Mom listened and followed it to the letter. "Yes, I'm here for the Lockwood party. My mother perhaps gave you the diet restrictions."

The server tapped his pencil on his chin before saying, "Most items are for tomorrow night, but we can whip up cheesesteak-stuffed peppers, or eggplant parmesan, or baked salmon with bacon butternut squash."

"They all sound wonderful. The salmon and squash, please." Jo grinned, the relief flooding through her. What a difference when people treated you as an adult rather than a sick child.

"Make it two, Javier, and a soda too, please," Brett said.

"Water for me," Jo added, and the server headed to the prep area. She looked at Brett, wanting to explain. "About the diet," she said, but he waved her off.

"No worries. Tons of people do the gluten-free thing. Eat what you like." He shrugged, taking a last sip of his beer.

His off-handed, pleasant manner made her want to explain even more. "I can't have it at all. I'm not just sensitive. I actually have celiac."

Brett raised his eyebrows, and embarrassment crushed her. *Talk about too much information.* Heat rose on her cheeks and neck.

"Sorry. I'm over sharing. I thought I..." She shook her head, her face blazing. "I'm kinda awkward about food. I've always had issues."

"Wait." He held up a hand. "You're going a little too fast for me. Start with the disease thing. Do we need an epi-pen if they feed you wrong, or what?" His gray-brown eyes filled with concern. "No wonder you didn't want to eat in here. Come on, we'll hit the lounge." He held out a hand.

"No, I'm fine. I'm allergic to gluten. It makes me ill, but I don't go into anaphylactic shock." His eyebrows knitted. "No epi-pen necessary. Only a bathroom and bed rest."

He scrubbed his chin as the server placed salads in front of them. "So, eating bread stuff makes you sick?"

She nodded. "Yeah, it took a long time to figure out my problem. I was sick most of my childhood. Celiac was rare, so they treated my migraines and seizures..."

"Seizures? Damn."

"Yeah, but once I received a diagnosis and good medical advice, I improved almost immediately. As long as I watch what I eat." She smiled, relief flooding her. Usually, she didn't share so much, but usually, she didn't eat with strangers. Most of her meals out comprised Mom hovering over her and barking orders at the wait staff. Blurting out her personal story warmed her all over. Hopefully, Brett didn't mind listening.

"So," he said, considering "Good thing I didn't ask you out for a beer."

"Coffee works better." She smiled, a genuine one that stretched to her toes. *He considered asking me for a drink? Yes!*

What if she brought him to the dinner party tomorrow night? She imagined them huddling together at a back table and making fun of Mom's friends.

They ate their salads in comfortable silence, no desire to fill the space with mindless chatter. He didn't seem like a small talk kind of guy, anyway.

After they'd eaten most of their dinners, Brett spoke up. "You told me something about yourself, and I've been trying to find something to share. But I'm boring. No stories to tell." He chewed his food and considered. "I'm here at the Excelsior to renovate old bathrooms. Stanley, the manager, and I are old buddies from way back. I'm not the regular handyman here."

"Oh," she said, feeling silly for her assumption, and then embarrassed she'd thought he was hotel staff.

"I thought I'd mention it." He paused. "I'm here till Saturday before I head back to my family's business in Stonewater. I live between there and Iverton. It's a nice place, small. I, uh... I guess that's it."

Unable to help herself, Jo laughed aloud. "Aren't we a pair? Now the conversation turns to our favorite movies, colors, and breakfast food, right?"

He laughed. "Well, it's weird. You practically froze to death today, and I almost saw you naked. I thought I'd share something, too."

"Brett, you are a breath of fresh air."

He furrowed his brow. "Why? 'Cause I'm blue collar and you're... not?"

She shook her head. "Because I don't have to be anyone but myself around you. It's nice."

"Well, that's good," he said with a grin. "I'd hate to eat dinner with you and find out later you were fake. Drinks tomorrow night wouldn't be as interesting."

"Drinks? Sounds wonderful. I have to go to my mother's party tomorrow, but I can sneak out."

He grinned. "I'll show you the work I've done to the old rooms. They need a total overhaul, but Stan wants the basics for now. So, we're focusing on the bathrooms."

"Do you do a lot of work like that?" *Fascinating. Someone who works with his hands rather than everyone doing it for him.* She loved the idea. Her gaze dropped to his hands. They were large and calloused. What they would feel like running over her skin? She shivered.

"Jo?" Brett asked, concern in his voice. Great, he was worried she'd eaten something bad.

"I'm fine. Just a chill."

"No, I asked about your work. You wandered off to dreamland for a second." He paused, his cheeks slightly pink. "Sooooo..." He drew out the syllable, "What do you do for a living?"

"Well, nothing right now." Except for the demo game she put all her hopes and dreams on. No one else knew. And how could she share when she hardly knew him? Better to hedge. "I'm working on a project I hope to sell." Almost the truth.

"Oh, man," he said, "That's tough. Nothing harder than trying to sell an idea to someone else. I have ideas for the family business, but getting Dad or my brother to listen is like pulling teeth. Maybe you could give me some pointers for talking to them." He finished the salmon on his plate while Jo stared at him.

Someone asked her help, her opinion on something? She could like this Brett guy. Perhaps more bold moves were in her future.

Chapter Five

Brett tried hard not to stare at the cutie across from him. He loved that she babbled as much as he, the whole situation awkward. She never mentioned the tub. In fact, she appeared to be fully recovered and warm. He'd used every ounce of his self-control not to climb in there with her.

Not that she was drop-dead gorgeous, but she had an air about her. Like spider silk. Delicate and beautiful, but stronger than steel. He wanted to know everything about her. So, the babbling benefitted him. He'd have to hit Google later to research gluten-free stuff. Hopefully, food was her sole restriction.

When the server offered dessert, she declined. Brett pouted. Dessert was the best part of the meals here. Plus, they had a full gym to work off the extra food after.

Or there were always other activities.

He'd behaved so far, stopped being a man-ho for the entire job, acting professional and focusing on work. It wasn't easy.

The place overflowed with choice women interested in spending the night with the handyman. One woman showed up at his room in only a bathrobe. Stanley would've killed him. The manager mentioned more work at the Excelsior if the renovation went well, but Brett's heart remained with the business at home in Stonewater.

The words Kramer and Sons warmed his heart. He enjoyed working for Dad and Ted. Too bad little brother, Ryan, didn't understand the joy of running the business as a family. Maybe someday he would. He'd returned to town and was employed by the city. Brett planned to take him out for a beer and give him the straight shit. Ryan'd come around, eventually. Then he'd work on Ted after the deal was done.

The three of them could take their little contracting business to fresh places, creating contacts in Albany, Utica, Schenectady. Hire some punk-ass kids and teach them how to build things instead of destroying themselves.

But tonight was about the nice young woman sitting in front of him. Her presence sent new thoughts through his head about settling down and starting his own family. He'd never experienced "The Whammy," as his father called it. But this might be it.

"You sure I can't interest you in dessert? Or at least a cup of coffee?" he asked, wanting the dinner to last a little while longer. He rarely shared a meal with a woman who actually ate and held up her end of the conversation. He felt like a grown-up.

Her cheeks flushed pink. Maybe she didn't want to go either. "I should get back to my project. I'm sure my mother won't give me much time to work on it this weekend."

Ah, an in. "Tell me more about your project. Is that why you were on a laptop? Are you some corporate mogul making huge business deals on the internet? Buying and selling the world with a click of the mouse?" He waggled his eyebrows. But hell, she could be doing exactly that.

She waved his words away. "Nothing like that. It's a programming project."

He blinked at her, waiting for more information, trying not to seem stupid about computery things. Computers weren't his forte, but he knew how essential they were for business. Some days he felt he'd been born in the wrong century. Dad still did everything by paper, but Brett hoped to break him of that habit soon.

She glanced around the room as if she were about to bare her soul in confession. "Nothing like that. I'm programming a sample piece for an online gaming company." She waved away her words, and something about her dismissive gesture hit him in the gut.

"That sounds awesome. What it's about?" Games were not his thing. After long hours using his body to work, playing on a computer or game system didn't appeal to him even slightly. Usually, he found a paperback—a western or spy novel. And in the fall, televised football cured all that ailed him. He'd played a little in high school, nothing serious. He didn't have the bulk to play defense the way he wanted. But a cold beer, a bag of chips, and the Giants constituted the perfect evening.

"It's a demo three-match game for adults, but I gave it a role-playing backstory. Choose your character and totems... like that."

"Oh?" He raised his eyebrows, his glass poised at his lips. Visions of X-rated computer games with sex, violence, and loud music rolled through his brain. But it didn't seem her style at all.

"Not 'adult' adult," she said, as if reading his mind. "I wanted to impress the company by designing fun for grownups, not kids. Role-playing, kinda. Anyway, it's complicated, and I just finished the workable version to submit as a sample of my abilities."

Serious businesswoman after all. He grinned. "Sounds great. Teach me to play sometime?"

Her head rose and her gaze met his. Her mouth hung open, and it seemed as if he'd put his foot in it. She never really invited him, but he'd walked right through that door anyway. Embarrassed, he glanced away, heat on his neck.

"Anyway—" he blustered...

...at the same time she said, "Really?" in a breathy gasp.

He looked at her sideways, a goofy grin on her face. "Uh, sure. I'm not much of a gamer. So if you can teach me, you've made a major accomplishment."

She bounced in her seat. "I'd love to show it to you some time. It's on my laptop, but..."

"Whoa," he said with a laugh. "I'm here until at least Saturday. Guess we'll have to plan another meet-up to try the game."

Red colored her cheeks. "Oh, yeah. I guess so. But I can show you now... if you want. You don't have to. We don't have to go upstairs. I have it with me." She slowed as she said the last sentence, realization crossing her expression. "I'm not inviting you to my room for anything..."

Brett laughed aloud, her innocence adorable. He couldn't tell if she was trying to pick him up or not. With her cute mannerisms, babbling conversation, and over sharing, he'd say yes in a heartbeat.

This is the sort of woman he should be with. Not running around with ladies who only wanted him for sex. None of his relationships ever lasted longer than a month or two. But this girl... This woman made the boring world of Upstate fun and exciting. He grinned at her bright red face.

"How about we grab some coffee out in the lounge and check out your game?"

Jo grinned. "Okay." She grabbed her laptop bag and dashed out of the kitchen, the door swinging in her wake.

Okay, then.

Guess he'd get to spend a few more minutes with the woman of his dreams.

Jo searched the lounge for a free table near an outlet. She'd never shown anyone the work in progress except the development team. She kept the project to herself, loving the independence of the secret. An open table sat in a corner, away from the riot of holiday decorations.

Perfect.

As she set up her machine, her brain whirled. Would he understand it? Was he being polite? Discovering someone, anyone, interested in her work warmed her heart. She'd willingly show him her baby.

Once the laptop was ready, she glanced up. Brett wasn't there. She scanned the room. Brett wasn't anywhere. Her stomach dropped.

Idiot.

She slapped her forehead. She'd dashed off without him. Tentatively, she stepped toward the kitchen, but leaving the computer alone on the table twisted her insides. She couldn't abandon it.

Brett exited the staff door a minute later, and guilt flooded through her.

The check.

She'd totally left him with the bill. In her universe, bills were never an issue. Mom handled everything, or her driver, or the nursemaid of the week.

Tonight had held infinite possibilities of fun and adventure—a meal with someone not on Mom's list, a conversation with someone interested in her and her work. There'd be no one hovering on Mom's every word or waiting for her permission. *Pure bliss.*

And she'd blown off the handsome handyman.

She bit her lip, unsure of what to do. Her mother would know the correct response to the situation, but she'd never let Jo talk to, much less hang out with, Brett in the first place.

He entered the lounge from the dining room, his head down as he examined his cell. He crossed the room as if on autopilot, stuffing his phone in his pocket. At her table, he put his hands out, palm up. "Hey, uh, Jo..." he began.

Against her will, words poured out. She didn't want to act like a child, like in the kitchen, but she couldn't stop herself. "I'm so sorry, Brett. I was so excited, and..."

He held up a hand to stop her—a large, calloused hand.

Focus.

"I gotta go," he said, his mouth in a straight line, grim. "I got a text I need to deal with. Sorry. I'll catch you later."

Her heart sunk as he left the room in a flash, his phone to his ear before he even made it out the door.

Gone.

No game, no conversation, no inviting him to her room later. No nothing.

Jo stepped back to her table, her fingers automatically reaching for the laptop, for comfort. A dark voice sounded in her head.

Mom.

Chapter Six

The plastic on the cellphone case creaked as Brett squeezed the device tighter.

Son of a bitch.

He couldn't leave town for one day without the universe blowing up. And to get it by text... Everything was going to pot. First, Ted was still a basket case, though Cheryl dumped him a year ago. Second, the serious lack of jobs in the fall and winter, and now...

He glanced at the texts again. Several from Ted, but only one from Dad. Neither contained good news.

Dad: *Fire at Porters. Not our fault. Gotta talk, but no need to come back.*

Curious, but Ted's...

Ted: *911... Need to talk NOW*

Thankfully, Ted added to his bizarre text in more cryptic half-sentences.

Ted: *shoulda texted earlier. Sorry. Fire at Earl's place. No one hurt. Ryan being a hero. But shit is going down.*

Brett's phone rang as he attempted to call Ted himself. "What's up?" he asked. "I got these texts, and..."

"I'm so pissed I can barely speak."

Brett pulled the phone away from his ear and glanced to ensure it was super-chill Ted. The guy had a long fuse, but when it reached the end, watch out.

"Calm down, bro. Tell me what happened." Brett paused outside the lounge, out of the flow of traffic.

"Did you hear about the fire?" Ted's words came out through heavy breaths, as if he'd been in the ring a few rounds before calling.

"Just your texts..."

And Ted launched into a tirade about a fire, Ryan, Dad, the business, everything. Apparently, Ryan put out the fire, investigated it, blamed Dad, then rescinded the blame. Brett's head spun. Ted moaned on through. Then, according to Ted, Dad turned the entire company, lock, stock, and barrel, over to their little brother without a word to the two older siblings.

Brett grimaced, pulling the phone away from his ear. Anger flared through him, white-hot. One of the desk twins strained her neck toward him, as if trying to eavesdrop. He narrowed his gaze and ducked into a stairwell for privacy.

Ted continued to ramble on, and it took a few minutes to get him back to earth.

"Bro," Brett repeated for the tenth time. "So, we didn't cause the fire?"

"No, but that..."

Brett broke through, tired of the sketchy details, but also trying to process what his brother communicated. "And Dad up and handed the entirety of Kramer and Sons to Ryan."

Ted sighed in relief. "Yeah."

"Well, fuck. Dad told me not to come home because you don't need me." Anger rolled over him.

"Well, no, I guess not." The trepidation in Ted's voice didn't quell Brett's anger one bit.

"Whatever," he snarled and ended the call.

They "didn't need him?" Seriously? Who cleaned all the messes lately? With Dad indifferent and Ted unfocused and lost, Brett covered for them more times than not.

He put some blame on Ryan coming back. The guy showed up out of the blue, back in town, and not working for Dad. It hit the man hard, not that he ever said anything. And there was Brett left holding the bag, getting no credit for keeping the family together.

With a curse at the lack of cell reception, he headed to his room. He tossed the phone on the bed and paced. He should head home and handle this, but he needed at least another day to finish the rooms. Abandoning the job now would piss off Stanley. No more winter work for the Kramers if Brett ditched now.

The room was too small to move in. With no more pressing texts, he considered his options. Nothing left to do but wait. But man, the pent-up energy gnawed at him. An image of Jo in the tub rose in his brain. An evening in her company would burn a few thousand calories if she...

His thoughts dropped off as he covered his face with his hands. He'd blown her off, left her hanging in the lounge with her computer fired up. She'd been so excited to share with him, and *boom*, he'd walked out.

He fell on the bed, the anger and extra energy gone. Damn his family, always fucking him one way or another. They always left him in the lurch and never gave him half a break. Ted, as the oldest, always pushed to be in charge, to be the leader. Too bad lately he couldn't find his way out of a paper bag. Women were always Ted's downfall, and Cheryl...

Hell, his brother needed to stay far away from the girl. Brett told him so at the beginning. She ripped his heart out and chewed it to pieces.

Then there was little Ryan, two years Brett's junior. The golden boy. Ry could do no wrong in Dad's eyes. Dad hadn't said a word when Ry took off east to the big city and left the business a man short—a trained and talented man who knew his shit. Brett and Ted tried to compensate for the loss, and Dad acted as if it was no big deal.

Now this mess.

Brett knew exactly which job started the clusterfuck—that asshole Earl Porter. Brett rolled over on the bed, considering. He'd helped with the job, but as he ended up being the emergency guy, he'd been pulled off to help with a broken hot water heater.

And Earl fired them. Dad let it go without a fuss. Brett argued until he lost his breath, but Dad filed the paperwork and moved on to the next job.

Dad quitting the business over it? And Ryan being chosen to lead the company after he'd abandoned them years ago? Seriously? And not a word from Dad? It chapped Brett's ass hard. Why now? It was fucking Christmas.

Not to mention, he'd blown off a beautiful woman because of the bullshit.

He remembered Jo's excitement at showing him her computer game. She seemed to have a genuine passion for it. He'd been a dick. He should go to the lounge and explain. Hopefully, she'd still be there. And he knew her room number.

Groveling usually worked. And maybe... With the excess energy shifting inside him, his thoughts went lewd.

No, dammit. She wasn't a booty-call kinda girl.

The best thing to do, as he always did with these crap situations, was hit the gym. He grabbed his duffle and changed, sliding his key card in his sock. Glancing at the phone, he opted to leave it behind. He could tolerate the canned music played over the loudspeakers for an hour.

After a grueling run and two rounds of weights, Brett rested on the bench. He didn't feel any better about the family situation, only tired. Grabbing a towel, he hit the shower and changed into clean shorts and a tank. He hated being sweaty and smelly after working. Headed to his room, he took the long way to enjoy the quiet of the hotel at night. Most people were tucked away in their beds, ready for tomorrow's winter fun—skiing, tobogganing, a horse-driven carriage through the snow. The lounge would be silent and dark except for twinkling lights on the two Christmas trees and the fireplaces.

The fireplaces... he loved them.

Something about the crackling fire, the lighting, and the warmth hit the spot. The dual hearths were the best feature of the hotel. The rest of the masses could take ski lessons, and play in the snow, but Brett loved nothing more than lounging in front of a warm fire with a beer and a book.

Quietly, he climbed the stairs to the main lobby. The night clerk raised a hand in greeting as Brett passed him. The large lounge stood in twilight. A few candles surrounded plastic pine wreaths dotted the tables. And in each fireplace, decked with subtle twinkling- lights, low embers glowed with a hint of flames licking the last of the logs. Stress leached out of his body better than during his workout. He moved among the leather furniture, seeking a nice high-back chair with a hassock near the flames.

He cursed, not bringing his cell or a book for something to read. He occasionally read on his phone, but paper always felt better. Besides, he loved bookmarking his spot and tipping the book on its side to see how much progress he'd made.

A glimmer of blue light caught his attention in the far corner. A computer. Brett's shoulders fell.

Jo sat by the corner, her head bowed over the machine, intent on her work.

Shame crept up his neck and hooded his face. He should talk to her, apologize, but what was the point? He wasn't trying for a hookup, and he'd been rude. Something in his chest fell. The love connection severed with a loud kaboom.

He glanced at the fireplace one last time, with an unexpected ache.

Jo.

He headed back to his room. If he stretched the renovation out one more night, he could indulge. Tomorrow was another day, another chance to reconnect. Unless Kramer and Sons needed him in Stonewater by morning.

Chapter Seven

At breakfast the next morning, Josephine kept an eye out for Brett. She owed him an apology or something. The entire thing seemed so awkward and strange. Her nerves were responsible for her reaction last night. Between the dinner party and the gaming contract, she didn't know up from down.

The party was more concerning than it should've been. Mom had been relentless lately. She amassed dozens of young people at various parties to socialize with Jo. All the while, Mom cautioned guests about being careful with touching and contact. As if Jo's celiac might get worse from a handshake or a sharing a meal.

Dexter Charlton appeared to be Mom's newest favorite. He visited the house several times a week, though he hardly ever spoke a word to Jo or she to him. Jo tried to date him, tried to form a close connection, but intimate contact sent him running for the hills. The one time she tried...

Eww, not going there.

She switched her thoughts back to the usual complaints about Mom. Like the job thing.

Pre-diagnosis, the woman had blurted out. "Josephine, how could you ever hold a job with your health issues? Everything sets you off, puts you in bed, or the hospital. We may never find out what's hurting you, sweetie. You need to plan for that. Plan for your future. However long that future is."

Before she gave up gluten, her health had gone from bad to worse as the effects of the celiac disease continued to ravage her body. Unknowingly eating the wrong foods day after day, she was slowly killing herself. At one point, during her college studies, she ended up in the hospital on an IV, her weight dangerously low.

She remembered the nurse, Jaime. The woman came into the room and locked the door behind her. She crossed to the bed and took Jo's hand in hers.

"Look," Jaime said. "I'm no doctor, but I've done rotation on the pediatric ward." Jo looked at her, confused. "You're no kid, but I glanced at your records. Honey, tell me right now. I won't judge, but I will get you help."

"What are you talking about?"

Jamie sighed and squeezed her hand. "There's a mental illness called Munchausen syndrome. Are you doing this to yourself?"

Jo blinked at her.

Jaime shook her head. "I didn't think so. Munchausen syndrome by proxy..."

"Like the old movie with the ghost-seeing kid?"

She nodded. "Is your mother doing it to you? It's less common between adults, but it sure looks like—"

Jo held up a hand to stop her. "No. I know it looks bad, but my mother... she wants to keep me safe, wants me to be protected. It isn't in her to hurt me. I'm her only child, and she just... well, she's so worried I'll leave her. She'd never injure me on purpose."

Jaime narrowed her gaze, her mouth in a tight line. "I'm not sure..." She shook her head. "I said something to the doctor, and he nay-sayed it. But it should be in your record somewhere. You should know. You should be vigilant." She pressed her lips as if holding back anger.

Jo swallowed and said, "Mom took a month-long cruise without me a few years ago. She arranged for me to stay at a spa during her absence. I could have stayed at the house, but she worried. I got sick there, too. In fact, I had a bad bout and went to the hospital. My mother isn't the cause."

Jaime shook her head, still not believing. "Just be careful, okay? Move out. Be super sure."

Jo listened and regulated her diet after that. She ate nothing Mom brought her. Sometimes she had difficulty faking it or hiding the food. But for a good solid two months, she managed and was still sick. A short time after she stopped watching Mom, her masseuse found the rash.

Jo reflected on Jaime's idea for a second. *What kind of person would...* She left the thought there. No use spending time on a nonissue. She turned back to her program.

A half an hour later, Brett hustled into the breakfast area and made a cup of coffee. Or he tried to. He looked left and right, his mouth dropping into a frown. Only tiny cups remained in the dispenser, and someone else had snagged the last from the large pot. Brett hung his head, teeth gnashing.

Jo sympathized with him. No coffee in the morning made her super cranky, too.

As she stood to help him, he wheeled and disappeared into the kitchen. She sat down, disappointed he hadn't noticed her.

After a minute, he reemerged with a large travel mug in his hand and a satisfied grin on his face.

Jo stared at him for a second, drinking in his expression. Something about his smile tickled her deep down. She would kill to see that smile as he hovered over her naked body.

Embarrassed and a little giddy, she shook off the sexy thoughts and crossed to the handyman. She'd steal a few minutes from his busy day. "Hey," she called softly as he headed for the door.

Brett stopped and glanced around, his brow furrowed.

Jo stepped forward, her hands crossed in front of her, her bottom lip caught under her teeth.

He smiled. "Hey, Jo. Sleep well?"

His voice sounded strained, as if he were as uncomfortable as she. Perhaps she'd read the situation wrong yesterday, imagined their connection. Maybe it was all in her head, and he hadn't really glanced at her with those bedroom eyes last night.

"Get your problem solved? You seemed kinda upset." She stepped to the side so as not to block the entrance to the dining room, and Brett mirrored her actions.

He scrubbed the back of his neck. "Uh, yeah. Business problems at home because of a fire."

Her eyes widened, terrible thoughts racing in her brain. A fire constituted the worst thing in the world for her.

"Not my place," he added hurriedly. "No one got hurt. It's... uh... complicated. I'm waiting to hear from my brother, but I gotta finish the job here." He shrugged, but worry remained in his eyes.

"Oh, I'm sorry. I just wanted to..." What the hell did she want to do? Here stood her hunk of a handyman, obviously frazzled with much on his mind, and she hedged and fawned over him. "I wanted to say thanks for dinner. I'm sorry I ran off and—"

"Oh, that." He laughed. "No worries. Nice to see someone so passionate about their work."

Her brow furrowed. "And you're not?" An opening to a conversation, but would he bite?

He shrugged. "About some parts, but..." He waved away the rest of his comment. "You don't wanna hear about the struggles of a family-owned business. Sorry I didn't see your project." He seemed genuinely apologetic.

"Another time." She smiled, trying not to seem too needy. Every fiber of her body wanted to rush him to her room and show him the game.

Naked.

She blinked as the enticing idea hit her full-on. She never behaved this way around men. Of course, most of the men she knew were wiggling their way into her mother's good graces, or her wallet.

Brett was a regular blue-collar guy. He didn't seem to care about her last name or her history of health problems. It was part of his appeal, the other being his broad chest and tight butt.

"I'll be in the lounge later, waiting for my mom's guests to arrive either today or tomorrow." She threw the comment out, not sure if she appeared too needy, too "come and see me." She wanted to show him but didn't want to be a nag.

"Your family?" his brow furrowed. "Oh, yeah. There's some party tomorrow night. The kitchen staff is buzzing about it."

"Just another of my mother's holiday parties. She likes to say she's doing these for me. But really, it's an excuse to be hostess. She's doing gluten-free. So when people complain about the menu..." She shrugged a shoulder, rolling her eyes.

"Don't worry too much, Jo." Hearing him speak her name sent electricity down her spine. "The cooks here are excellent. I bet it'll be the best dinner you've ever had." He grinned. "I gotta go. Toilets and sinks to install. Boring, but must be done."

"See you." Jo watched as he headed to the opposite wing of the building. She studied his butt as it moved in those jeans. She'd ask him to her room today or tonight or something. He might say no, or it might be the boldest decision of her life.

Brett hummed as he installed the new bathroom fixtures in an ancient room. Stan needed to update more than bathrooms. The section required new carpets, beds, furniture, everything. Even Brett realized it was old, outdated, and unflattering. And he had no aesthetic abilities whatsoever.

Kramer and Sons couldn't do much for the place, other than paint and install new carpet. Stanley might pass a recommendation on to the owner if he did an outstanding job. A dozen sad rooms stood empty, which could only be filled with last-minute arrivals, or temp staff like him.

He sat back, admiring the work—a no-brainer job, but satisfying, nonetheless. And it let his mind wander over and over to a certain young lady in a bathtub. The woman kept sneaking into his head since he first laid eyes on her. And not the almost-flashing in her bathroom. Dinner had been great, and *she'd* apologized for *him* taking off to talk to Ted. He should make it up to her, visit her room, view her project, give her multiple orgasms.

That made him chuckle. She might be game. She'd been giving him that come-hither vibe since he met her. But women like her didn't want guys like him for much more than those multiple orgasms.

And damn it, he would not play those games here.

Stan watched him like a hawk, and Brett hoped his womanizing label wouldn't follow him into another town.

Yes, he dated a bit. And most relationships didn't last long. But he wasn't the hook-up king his brothers made him out to be. He liked sex, but not relationships. He behaved like a complete gentleman to the woman for the twenty-four to forty-eight hours he spent with them. And then he moved on.

But Jo was different, and not because she booked the Presidential Suite for a few days. The chatter he'd heard about the Christmas party sounded both ominous and ridiculous. He didn't listen to gossip, and being temporary help, he didn't know the staff well. But tidbits dropped here and there, especially from those clerks at the front desk. Talk about drama queens.

He checked his phone again. No more messages from Ted or Dad. Texting Ryan would be annoying. The two hadn't talked much since his little brother returned to town.

When Ry chose to work for the town rather than the business, Brett was beyond pissed. Ryan always sat so high and mighty, acting better than the rest of the family. Brett had no use for his spoiled-brat attitude. Kramer and Sons was good enough for Dad, Ted, and himself. Why didn't Ryan climb off his high horse and help them out?

Most annoyingly, Ryan had impressive skills in construction. He knew how to complete most jobs without a consult or hiring out. He'd learned it by watching his big brothers and father. Dad made all three of them work for the company for years. But Ryan bugged out to Albany and landed himself in a terrible mess.

Maybe it was better this way.

Anyway, Dad or Ted would message him soon enough. Once he finished the bathrooms, he'd head home and get the story straight from the source. Porter fired them, so the fire probably had nothing to do with Kramer and Sons. But Earl, the dick, might not see it that way. The cost of a lawyer would be an ugly expense in the winter. Maybe he'd feel out Stanley for more work, stay a little longer.

Or get invited to the Christmas party with Jo.

He stopped his wrench in mid-twist.

Where the hell did that come from? Sneaky, meaningless sex was one thing, but attending a family event with a girl he'd just met? He shivered from head to toe. He'd need a suit or something better than his ripped jeans and flannels. Plus, he brought nothing fancy to the hotel. The round trip to grab his funeral suit wasn't worth any party. Besides, if Jo wanted to invite him, she'd had plenty of opportunities.

Her innuendoes hinted at sex, never the party. He ran his tongue over his teeth. Could be that Jo saw him as good enough to screw, but not good enough to meet her family?

Meet her family?

He grumbled under his breath. He'd met the woman, talked to her two—no, three times, and now he fantasized about being introduced to her circle.

Best to put his head down and get the work done. If he rushed, he could leave before her little party tomorrow, not see her in an amazing, fancy dress, and have to deal with the blue balls at home.

Chapter Eight

Brett crossed the lobby at noontime. The two giggling clerks whispered as he walked by. Again he ignored them. He'd bet if he turned and talked one or the other up, he'd have a lunch date in a heartbeat, but they weren't worth the silly games and sad one-sided sex. The idea of intimacy manifested an image of Jo in his mind. *Pretty, delicate Jo dressed as a dominatrix.* He shivered and walked on to the kitchen, his gaze on his phone.

And because his head was tipped to the phone, he didn't see Jo and almost ran her down. She let out a "Whoa," which brought Brett up short. Her hands flew out to stop him, and he tried to skid to a halt. As a big guy, he couldn't stop on a dime. In an effort not to crash into her, he shot out his hands, sending his phone flying.

The two stood nose-to-nose, hands on each other's chests, panting. When Brett realized where his palms landed, he stepped back, snapping his arms behind his back. Heat burst out on his face, his phone forgotten.

"Jo," he said, startled, noticing she'd moved away from him, her head down. "I'm sorry. I wasn't watching."

She said nothing, although her chest vibrated, and her mouth quivered.

"Jesus, did I hurt you? Sorry. I didn't mean to grab—uh, touch—uh..." He scrubbed his fingers through his hair. "I mean, sorry."

Finally, she spoke, "I don't know whether to laugh or to slap you." Her voice filled with mirth. When she tipped her head to meet his gaze, they both burst into laughter. "Being around you makes for an interesting day, Brett Kramer."

He grinned. Her words created a warmth in him that went beyond a hormonal reaction to pure inspiration. Why couldn't he ask a woman like her out? Yeah, different social circles, economic circles, and they didn't live in the same town. But she was cute and didn't mind when he played Neanderthal. They could work. Another dinner like last night, and...

Her words cut into his daydream. "...regular repair or..." She caught his gaze and from her frown, she knew he hadn't been listening.

"Sorry," he said again and paused. Where did his phone go? He'd been reading the text from Dad about the situation in Stonewater. He glanced around. "You seen my phone?"

Jo's frown deepened. "Guess I can ask the desk." She walked past him, her nose in the air. *What was her problem?*

"Hey," he called after her. "I said I was sorry."

"And I asked you a question," she replied flatly. "Which you ignored." Her back stiffened more, and it rattled his cage.

Okay, yeah, he'd been a little rude yesterday, not seeing her project, not going over to her late that night. But he had no obligation here. He wasn't hotel staff and didn't have to kiss her ass. And they had sparks, but nothing more, despite sharing a meal.

"Please excuse me," he said, keeping the sarcasm out of his tone. With his best customer service voice, he continued, "I didn't mean to ignore you. I lost my phone when we crashed. It's kinda important to my business."

Jo glanced at him over her shoulder, a twinkle of mischief in her eye. "You were not thinking about your phone, mister."

Bold girl.

Was she always like this?

"No," he said, shifting closer as to whisper in her ear, "But I can't announce in the middle of the lobby that I was undressing you with my eyes."

If she could be bold, so could he.

Head down, she shielded her eyes with her hand. "I only wanted to ask if you knew how to fix the Wi-Fi." Her face shone scarlet, and Brett regretted teasing her.

He stood back, put his hands on his hips, and let out a belly laugh. "Of course, I meant the Wi-Fi. What did you think I was...?"

Her pursed lips and a scathing look stopped his joking. He'd like to take a few weeks—no, months—to figure out this mystery woman.

He gave her a tiny bow. "I'm not the hotel maintenance guy. I'm helping Stanley out, but the regular guy is around here somewhere. He probably..."

Jo didn't let him finish his statement. "Oh, I forgot." She faced him, her back to the registration desk, where the two clerks strained their necks to watch and hear the conversation.

Brett frowned at them but didn't want to start a war. Gently, he grasped Jo's arm and steered her away from the desk.

"Help me find my phone?" he asked, his gaze darting to the giggly girls.

Jo seemed to read his meaning. "Of course. I'm so sorry you dropped it." Her tone sounded pure blueblood, but a playfulness colored her smile. Brett fought not to laugh aloud. He liked Jo more and more every second he spent with her.

They began searching the room, edging away from the desk. He spotted the damned thing under a potted plant, face up. Hope sprung in his chest that he hadn't smashed the screen.

"Oh, here it is," Jo said, bending to pick it up. "Oh, dear." She held out the cell. "There's a crack."

Not what he needed right now. *Please let it be minor.* He didn't have a new phone in the budget. A flip phone might be affordable, but he loved his Android. And no Black Friday deals for about eleven months.

Cautiously, Jo handed it to him. Her entire body language said it might blow up at any second. He grabbed the device and examined it. A crack ran down the screen, but it still seemed functional. He pressed a few icons to be sure.

"Not too bad," he said, his brain calculating the cost of a screen versus a new cell.

"You sure? I can replace it." Her words sounded tentative, her shoulders by her ears. *What a disaster.* Nice, cute girl in the hotel. And every time they interacted, something stupid made it awkward. Now she offered to replace the phone he dropped when he ran over her, same as last night when she apologized for him running off.

Maybe it was a pattern with her. Always taking the blame and trying to fix things. Keep things smooth. Sounded similar to his job in his family.

The thought caught Brett unaware, and he huffed out a "huh" as he looked from her to the phone. She seemed to misinterpret the sound and lobbed out a sincere and sweet apology before he could stop her.

"Jo, I broke it. Don't try to fix my stupid. You'll end up poor with worry wrinkles." He flashed a lopsided grin, the one that always worked on the ladies at the clubs. He wasn't picking her up, merely putting her at ease.

Jo blinked at him. Something about his words struck her hard. "Don't try to fix my stupid." Hadn't that been much of her life—compensating for her illnesses, apologizing to everyone for being tired, sore, and sick?

And last night, she'd worried needlessly about the gluten thing. And Brett didn't care. Not an ounce. He didn't offer to do crazy things to get her food right. Or worry incessantly after she ate it. Hell, he hadn't stuck around to baby her one bit.

She kinda liked that.

Mom repeatedly took over her life, doing everything for her. She never let Jo lift a finger and worried all the time. Twice a week, she'd lay the guilt on thick about how she'd given everything up for the girl. If her mother had witnessed Brett plow into her in the lobby, the man would be in handcuffs, and Jo, on a fainting couch with a blanket and water, with someone fanning her. But Brett apologized and blew it off, despite grabbing her chest.

It was almost... exciting.

A stupid grin crawled across her lips before she could repress it. "Okay, so you're not the regular repair guy, right?"

Eyebrows raised, Brett shook his head. He glanced at the broken phone again before shoving it in a pocket. If he wasn't worried, she shouldn't worry. But guilt bubbled inside her. She wanted to replace it, but people can be particular about their phones. She gave up in frustration.

"So, where is the guy? The Wi-Fi is down, and I need internet." The signal had dropped just after she'd hit Send on her sample program. With no internet, there was no way to confirm the submission. Her victory celebration turned in to a run down to the lobby.

But now, she had a plan. She'd fix the cable herself, a simple task, and only a matter of access.

Brett shrugged. "I don't know." He hesitated. "I guess I can help. It's my lunch break, and—"

"Oh, no, then. No, I won't take up your break with my issues." She turned to the desk, and he grabbed her arm.

"Having no Wi-Fi in the hotel is everyone's problem. We'll see what the deal is, and if we can fix it." They both sauntered over to the counter, their expressions identical, which thrilled Jo to no end. Their faces said, "We take no shit," and it snuffed out the smug looks on the clerk's face.

"Excuse me, miss." Jo used her best impression of Mom. "There seems to be no Internet access in the lounge or my room. How can we remedy the situation?" Brett turned his laugh into a cough, and she gave him a slight elbow to the ribs. "I require access for my work."

"Oh, let me see," Little-Miss-Full-of-Herself said. She seemed cowed by Brett's presence and Jo's attitude.

Jo never did this.

Ever.

She always tried to be polite, kind, and understanding. But the clerk constantly giggled at her behind her back. Especially when Brett was around. Jo had no time or use for silly kid games. *Do your job, do it well* was her motto.

"We've gotten calls already. I'll get Stanley." The clerk walked to the back office, but not before giving a weird look to Brett. She should know he wasn't regular staff. Jo considered the situation when Stanley came out of his office.

"Miss Lockwood, my deepest apologies. Ernie is working on an electrical problem near the server room. He's shut off power to the station for a bit. The internet will be up and running in a few hours."

Jo frowned. Why didn't the clerk tell her that? And for that matter, the hotel probably didn't have an actual server room. Just a router somewhere. She glanced at Brett, who took the lead.

"Hey Stan, want me to look at it?" Brett seemed open and laid back, but Stanley's stare gave off a skeptical air. "I'm on lunch, so no extra charge." Brett emphasized the last three words, his voice lowering, his chin set.

Jo wanted to argue, but anything hostile might hurt the awkward dynamic going on here. Her presence appeared to make Stanley ill at ease. She stepped back slightly, letting Brett's presence be the focus.

"I don't know," Stanley began, "Ernie..."

Brett stepped right up. "Ernie'd love having me cover for him. You know how he is. His plate is wicked full. And no

Wi-Fi makes everyone nutty. Let me look before we call the cable guy."

A service call this late on Friday wouldn't happen, and Jo needed the connection. Her phone didn't get enough signal for a decent hotspot. Her mother would kill her if she disappeared to a coffee shop or another hotel for internet.

Stanley and Brett chattered back and forth for a few minutes. Jo stayed back, not wanting to be a nosy guest. But she listened with one ear. Something about an electrical issue and fuses blowing. She grinned with a good idea of the actual situation.

Once Stanley gave them permission, Brett rested a hand on Jo's arm and steered her out of the office to the elevators. "Look," he said in a whisper. "I don't think we can get it working again soon. Ernie's busting a nut..."

Jo grimace at the raw term.

Brett frowned. "Oh, oops, sorry. Anyway, he's trying to fix the electrical in the ballroom for a Christmas party. Yours, right?"

"Kinda." Her mother's. But why split hairs?

"Will someone be a bear if everything isn't perfect?"

Jo hid her smile. "Yeah, Momma Bear has serious issues when things don't go her way. Trust me. But let's go check it out." She elbowed his ribs. "We might find something. After, I'll treat you to lunch."

Brett's face lit up at her words. Ah, food—the way to a man's heart. Or was it the prospect of eating with her? She hoped so.

"Can't hurt to look. The electrical's off. And I gotta warn you. I'm cursed." He tipped his head toward the hallway leading to the ballroom.

"Cursed, how?" She raised an eyebrow. "You aren't one of those people who give constant shocks and break everything with a battery?" Visions of her laptop blowing up invaded her head. She needed the internet to put her project on the cloud. Her flash drives contained room for a full backup and then some. But if he gave off electric shocks, he might blow those out, too.

"No, not me. The stuff with my family yesterday." He held up the cracked cell. "My brother is causing more problems from the original problem, the fire, which wasn't our fault. He's the town building inspector."

"Isn't that a conflict of interest? Being related to the contractors? That's not a problem?"

Brett laughed, a full belly laugh. "Not in my family. Ryan's the perfect everything. No one questions his integrity. Ever." He chuckled, "Fucking Ryan."

Jo pursed her lips. "Little brother?" she asked.

Brett snorted. "How d'ya guess?"

"I know a few things about family dynamics. I've observed much from my sickbed." She elbowed him again. "You gonna blow up the ballroom for the party? Because I wouldn't mind one bit."

Brett stopped mid-stride, his jaw opened wide. He slapped his hands to either side of his face. "You might miss the big fancy party! What will you do?"

She giggled, loving his silly side. "Guess I could stay in my room and code." She shrugged.

"You do too much of that, sunshine. Let's get your Wi-Fi back so you can code and go to the party." He resumed his trek down the hallway, examining doors as he went.

"Wait, I'm not sure I thought it through. Maybe if the power isn't working, Mom will cancel the party, and I can go home." Jumping in the air, she gave a little whoop, thinking about abandoning it all for more *Adventures in Dining with Brett*.

He stopped at a door marked STAFF, his hand on the knob. "You wanna leave?" Disappointment colored his words as if he'd never see her again. Because she didn't say goodbye, or give him her number, or...

She paused in her celebration. "I want to get away from my mother, Brett. Not you." She said the words quietly, her hand resting on his arm. His gaze lowered to hers, a slight smile on his lips. He shifted closer, their bodies inches apart.

"She's not here now," he said. The first real invitation he'd given her. Jo assumed he'd put her in the friend zone, but the sparks in his gaze said something else. Her body temp rose ten degrees as she leaned forward.

"No, she's not."

Chapter Nine

Brett knew he shouldn't do it, but there was something about Jo. Quirky and repressed, but she read him easily and apparently found nothing lacking. She didn't fawn over his body or looks. She talked to him like a real goddamned adult and only flinched when he swore.

He'd promised Stanley no hookups, but the situation seemed something else entirely. They clicked. He liked her. She was the one leaning in, not him. It was pretty clear she liked him for more than his blond hair and muscular arms.

Her angel face tipped to his, her eyes closed, her mouth ready.

With a breath, he leaned down to kiss those perfect lips.

Go slow.

A lifetime on bedrest made her virginal, at best, an actual virgin most likely—a woman he could take his time with and have a real romance.

That thought brought sweat to his forehead. Still, she waited for his kiss. The two seconds it took him to meet her mouth seemed like hours. Gently, slowly, he brushed his lips against hers, no pressure, a feather touch. His god-damned toes curled at the sensation of her delicate skin touching his. Why hadn't he shaved today?

Cursing his stupidity, he paused. She hadn't moved an inch or responded an iota.

Fuck.

He'd screwed it up. He gazed at her, waiting, wanting to throw her over his shoulder and run her to his room.

Her eyes opened, looking a little wild, and her gaze locked on his mouth. In a lightning move, not unlike a cobra strike, she grabbed the back of his head and crushed her mouth to his. Walls crumbled in that kiss. No more hesitating. No more guilt for seeing her wet in her bathrobe.

Damn. It's on...

Then the staff door smacked him in the ass, driving him forward, right into Jo. He threw his hands out, wrapping one around her waist, the other out to catch the wall. His shoulder smashed into the doorframe opposite, sending red sparks up his arm. But Jo remained cradled and safe in his grip. Her feet slipped out from under her, but she didn't hit the floor.

"You okay?" he asked.

A voice sounded behind them. "That you, Brett? Stanley said you'd be down. Whatcha doing making-out in the hallway?"

Ah, Ernie.

Good guy, but not the sharpest tool in the chest.

"Hey, Ernie," he said, setting Jo on her feet. Her face flushed scarlet again. He loved that. "I was looking for you."

Ernie snorted. "Yeah, sure you were."

Brett stared at him stone-faced, and Jo hid behind him. He let her, though he hated her not bold in the face of idiocy.

Ernie's grin disappeared in a heartbeat.

"Trouble with the power?" Brett clipped his words to inform Ernie he would not bullshit around here.

Ernie's hands dropped into his pockets, his expression sobered. "Yeah, the ballroom ceiling leaked and tripped a breaker. I'm trying to find the source of water. Probably an ice dam, but it's making the lights spark in that section."

Brett nodded. *I should duck into the ballroom to view the damage.* Jo's hand squeezed on his arm as if she'd read his mind. "Bad?" He crossed his arms, hating that the action removed her hand.

Ernie shrugged. "I got time to figure it out, so..." His slack expression said he didn't plan to work hard to remedy the situation.

"So," Brett said, scrubbing his chin. "You have an ice dam—roof work and sparking electrical that needs time to dry. You shut off the electricity to this part of the building." He waved at a dark light fixture.

"Eh, it's noon. Plenty of time." Ernie snuffed, gesturing to the room he just exited. "That bitch won't know nothing."

Jo stiffened.

Anger and disappointment flared in Brett's chest. *Never bad-mouth a client. Never blow off work because you've "got time."* Nine times out of ten when fixing something, an additional problem sprung up. A good contractor, a good repairman understood the delicate nature of the universe, and how any job could turn to shit at any second. So attack and hope the problems aren't worse than you expected.

"Let me introduce you to Jo Lockwood, the bitch's daughter."

Ernie's face fell.

"So, maybe you want to get on the ballroom problem ASAP, huh?"

Ernie dashed into the staff room and ran back out, tools in hand. He flew down the hallway at breakneck speed and slammed through the double doors.

Jo pressed against his arm. "You think he'll fix it?" She sounded distant. Not amazed or awed by Brett's authority, but wistful.

"You don't want to go to the party?"

She shook her head. "But I also don't want Mom mad the room isn't perfect, or..." She waved away the words, and a single tear ran down her cheek.

Brett caught his breath. "Damn, I'm sorry. Let me grab a sandwich, and I'll make sure the room is perfect by the time..."

Placing a hand on his arm, she stopped his speech. She leaned her head against him. "No, don't kill yourself for this. When she's not happy, it can get ugly. I don't want her taking it out on either you or Ernie. Mom doesn't understand shit happens." She giggled as she swore, putting delicate fingers over her mouth.

"But the party... it seemed kinda important. The staff has been hustling..."

"For a woman with a big budget." She glanced at him, gray eyes rolling in their sockets. "Let's fix the Wi-Fi so the entire hotel can have internet access. Let Ernie take care of the items for the party." Her smile didn't hit her eyes.

"Come on," he said. "The 'server room' should be in here." He opened the door to a dark room full of electrical cables, machines, and tools. "Shit," he remarked. "There's no power in here either."

Jo entered the room. "I got this. First, we find the cable modem and move it." She flipped her flashlight app on.

"The what?" He understood the basics of computers, like how important it was for business. He could wire a kitchen, call up a picture of a contract on his phone, but websites, routers, and such were beyond him.

Jo shone her flashlight here and there, touching one machine or another. "I can see why they think it's the server room. Someone set up a mancave, probably Ernie."

"Mancave?" A word he knew. How did it apply to computer things?

Jo giggled, raising her arms to the side to indicate the entire room. "There's an MMO station here." She hit a key on a still-running machine. "This one's on battery power." She clicked a few things and smirked.

"What?" He hated not knowing things, especially for electrical stuff. His dad held a state certificate and taught him everything about wires and power.

"That same someone has been playing internet games while on break. But it's no server room. The hotel's not in the data business. But that's a nice-looking cable modem. The building has repeaters throughout."

She crouched in front of a box that looked as dead as a doornail. "We'll just move it." She picked up the box. Its cables didn't have much slack. "Can you unhook this?"

"Uh, I guess." He touched his tool belt, unsure.

"Just a few co-ax cables."

Co-ax? Now she was talking his language.

Jo studied the machine. Easy to move. She stepped back, allowing Brett access to the device.

His concerned expression disappeared as he pulled a wrench from his tool belt. "So we unhook this. Then what happens?"

"Where can we hook it up? Any cable access will do."

"So, it's just... another co-ax in? Nothing magical or computery?" He looked mystified.

Jo hid a smirk. People always thought the computer universe was mystical. In reality, it was just wires, electricity—ones and zeros.

He handed her the liberated modem, doubt in his expression.

"Trust me, Brett."

He shrugged. "What's next?"

That simple statement stole her breath away. Every fiber of her being wanted to kiss him again. Kiss him until they both exploded. He trusted her. No coddling, no telling her "women don't understand these things." Not saying she couldn't know something he didn't.

She'd never met a man like him. Every guy Mom paraded in front of her tried to control her, run her life as Mom did. They always assumed she was a fragile flower on a pedestal. Someone who required special care, with no brain of her own.

Tears filled her eyes. She placed a hand over her mouth, afraid a sob or hysterical laughter might erupt from her lips.

His brow furrowed. "Did I break it? Man, I'm sorry. I thought it was like any other cable connection. Fuck." He slammed the wrench into his tool belt.

"No, no. Nothing like that. We need the router, too." She pointed to the device. "And the cables connecting the two, an ethernet cable."

Brett looked at her dumbly, and she patted his arm. She reached over, unplugged the machine from the outlet, and unhooked the ether cable. She wound the cords and glanced around, making sure they grabbed everything.

"Now to hook it up."

"You tell me where, because I have no clue." He held his hand out for the router and cables. She didn't want to give them up, but Brett was being chivalrous. She let him.

"How about Stan's office?"

"Oh man, he'll love that."

They headed from the "server room" to the lobby. The giggle twins disappeared from the desk, replaced by a stout middle-aged woman. She raised an eyebrow at the two of them and all the computer equipment.

"Can I help you?" she asked, skepticism darkening her words.

"Can we get into Stanley's office?" Brett asked, holding up the modem. The clerk didn't seem impressed.

"No," she said flatly. "Mr. Frasier is out, trying to deal with the roof leak." The phone next to her rang. "You can wait there for him." She pointed to a bench as she grabbed the handset.

Jo glanced at Brett, who shrugged. *Oh no, we're not giving up that easily.* She tapped on the registration desk, examining the room as she listened in on the call.

"Yes, we are aware of the internet issue. The roof has a leak... Well, I'm not sure how it stops the Wi-Fi. I'm aware it's down... Yes, ma'am. As fast as we can... no, we won't compensate."

Jo leaned over the desk. Two dozen messages littered the space. Most labeled with "No internet."

"Psst," she hissed at the clerk, who gave her a startled and annoyed look. "Let us in the office, and we'll fix the Wi-Fi."

The clerk's mouth dropped open as her hand slackened on the phone receiver. "Really?" she asked, the handset pressed to her chest. "Don't screw with me here. I got a million calls about..."

Jo placed a hand on the counter. "We need access and five minutes. You know Brett." He gave legitimacy to their request. Jo figured her presence would cinch it. "I'm Josephine Lockwood."

The woman fluttered, dropping the handset. "Oh, quick, please." She gestured toward the closed door of Stanley's office.

Jo grinned as she rounded the desk and opened the door. "Cable access?" she asked Brett, who hustled in behind her.

"Oh, he has a cable hookup here somewhere. Who do you think previews the adult films?" He waggled his eyebrows.

"Eww." She scrunched up her nose, stepping away from the counter.

"Eww, indeed."

In two minutes flat, Jo set up the cable modem on Stanley's desk with the router next to it. The lights flashed and blipped for a second before falling into a steady rhythm. Brett looked at her expectantly.

A bead of sweat rolled down her neck. The installation of a cable modem amounted to a simple thing, but a pressure built in her chest, regardless. It seemed like her entire relationship with Brett depended on the Wi-Fi running correctly now.

A slight nervousness floated over her as she pulled out her phone. "Guess we should check, huh?"

He shrugged. "I usually test the reliability of my work. But you do what you need." He winked at her. His confidence rolled over her like a warm blanket. He believed in her. He let her fix the problem without chastising, giving advice, or doing it for her. With a sigh of relief, she clicked phone settings and hit the login for the hotel Wi-Fi.

And it worked.

One click, and she was in. She hit her browser and searched for a few random topics to be sure new content came through. The pages loaded every time.

She beamed. "Seems to work. How about you?" She regretted the words as soon as they passed her lips. She'd broken his phone with the run-in. "Wait, never mind..."

Brett shook his head. "One little crack. Seriously? Calm yourself." His words made her laugh, genuinely laugh. With Brett, she didn't need to adhere to strict high-society rules, to formality and uber-politeness. He took her at face value every time. And the kiss... she couldn't think about the kiss.

Her thoughts trailed off as she gazed into Brett's eyes. A new light shone in them.

"Damn, you did it. Well done. We'll check with the clerk and find out if the system is up building-wide."

"We should go to my room and check my laptop," Jo said in a dreamy voice.

Brett's gaze snapped to hers. "All right." The words came out on a cool breath, his eyes turning dark. Didn't have to hit the guy over the head when trying to seduce him. He got it in one.

Chapter Ten

Josephine could not believe her audacity. Inviting a man she'd just met to her room for they both knew what. They hurried by the reception clerk, telling her the internet access was back, and rushed to the elevator.

Brett paused at the closed door; his gaze raked her body up and down. One edge of his lip curled in a half-smile.

She wasn't used to such scrutiny. Usually, she hid in the corner, away from the spotlight. But Brett's gaze stirred something deep inside. She looked at him—really looked.

He was hot and kind of goofy. Sweet, too. He never played the stud, not to her or the giggle twins at the desk. He was a gentleman when he rescued her. The memory of his hands on her as he carried her to the tub sent a thrill down her spine.

The elevator slid open, and they stepped inside. Once the door closed, Jo inched toward him, and he met her halfway. Their arms around each other, their faces millimeters apart. He paused, and her lips ached to touch his.

"You sure?" he asked, breathy, his baritone vibrating her body.

She closed her eyes and let it all sweep over her. This day, this man... "Oh, yes," she moaned, and his lips fell on hers.

Electricity danced across her skin as his lips first brushed hers, then pressed. A kiss so perfect, so careful, and wanting at the same time. He let her lead. She tried to hold back, be a lady, but inside her, an animal roared. She opened her lips and devoured him.

The elevator dinged, and the door opened. Reluctantly, Jo broke the kiss, her gaze rolling up to his devilish grin. She needed to get him in her room, fast.

The distance down the hall to her suite seemed a thousand miles, but also a single step. At the double door, she fiddled with the key, her fingers trembling.

"Here, let me," he said, taking the card. The simple brush of his fingers against hers sent vibrations throughout her body. Her knees weakened, and she clutched his arm for support. More contact sent more tingles.

He swiped the card, ushered her inside, and closed the door behind them with a snick of the lock.

She and Brett—alone in her room. *My God...*

Jo pressed her lips, glancing at the floor.

"Everything okay?" he asked.

"Yeah, random thought." She stepped toward him, wanting to tell him how much she desired him. She stood before him, hands on his shoulders.

"Brett," she said, breathless.

His gaze raked over her face once more before he lowered his lips to hers. Slowly, he nudged her backward until her legs hit the bed, and she sat.

He stood over her, staring with a heat that put goosebumps on her skin.

Her lips parted slightly. She wanted to say... say what?

Gazes still locked, he pulled his shirt off, his head cocking to the side as he dropped the garment to the floor. His chest was romance-cover perfect. Men built muscles from either hours of working out, or a life of hard work. Jo guessed Brett did a bit of both.

A flutter of nerves coursed up her skin. He was perfect, too perfect. Doubt and trepidation raced in her brain. She frowned.

It was a terrible idea. She hardly knew him. He could be a raging alcoholic, or a Republican.

Teeth gritted, she pushed those thoughts aside. Brett had been nothing but nice. One night with him might help put her life in perspective.

"You okay?" His voice sounded husky, but Jo noted he asked permission. And considering his pants were getting tighter by the second, Jo gave him full points for gentlemanliness.

Plus, yay for thin khakis.

"One second." He dashed back toward the door and knelt by his tool belt. Jo got a delightful view of his tush in those tight pants. Beautiful. She could eat breakfast off that butt.

Turning back, he flashed a foil package.

"You keep condoms in your tool belt?"

"You got a better place for them?" He walked over to the bed and tossed it on the night table. He towered over her again, and a streak of heat coursed through her body. *Tall, handsome, and a little intimidating.*

She sat up, feeling brave enough to pull off her top. With a twist and a turn, and some assistance from Brett, she shed her shirt. After giving him a long blink, she flopped on the bed on her stomach, feeling a little exposed. Then she realized her mouth was inches from his crotch. Heat seeped into her cheeks, but she opted to go with it. Tipping her head back, she gazed at him.

A small smile touched his lips. His eyes locked on hers, he unbuttoned his pants and let them drop to the floor.

Jo swallowed hard. It was too much, but Brett was... well, he was every fantasy come true. Every romance hero, every superhero, every dream man wrapped into one. She wanted him, but perhaps she asked for too much, too fast.

She met his gaze, and a softness blurred over his expression.

He pressed his lips and cocked his head. With a gentleness no man with such a ripped chest should possibly have, he stroked her hair, and she shifted. It was too much. *How could I ask for this? How could I want this kind of intimacy after just a few days? How could a man like him want a woman like me? What was I thinking?*

He read the balk in her body language. "Jo..." The word held understanding and accommodation, with lust coloring its edges a deep crimson.

Something inside her opened up. She deserved wild passion. She deserved Brett. Something clicked in her head, and she transformed into another woman, a bold one who took want she wanted from her lover.

Before he could move away, she reached over and grasped the elastic of his jockeys. Letting it snap back, she said, "Don't leave yet." She pushed as much sexy into her voice as possible.

"Well, now..." He grinned and lowered his underwear, the back first, letting the fabric in front cling to his erection rather seductively.

A flutter of fear and excitement passed over her, like nothing she'd ever experienced before. Usually, sex occurred in the dark with a blueblood idiot who was too eager or too scared. Brett was pure confidence, all man, and she wanted him, wanted to do things she'd never done before.

She grabbed the tortured fabric and pulled it down with enthusiasm. His cock bent with the cloth for a brief second before springing back right before her face. Her attention focused on the most perfect eight inches she'd ever seen. The compulsion to be naughty ran over her again. On impulse, she planted a warm kiss on the top of the head. He gasped but didn't pull away.

Boldness rolling over her, Jo cautiously opened her mouth and took some of him in. He tasted like heaven. Her shyness and inexperience dropped away, and she gave Brett her all. Considering she'd only done this once before with minor success, he seemed to enjoy himself.

He ran his fingers through her hair. "Damn, Jo," he whispered as she grazed him with her teeth.

The feeling of fullness, knowing he was completely at her mercy, spurred her on to try other things—flicking her tongue on the head, letting him go deep, and a little hum here and there.

It wasn't long before he tugged at her hair. "Jo, you better slow down if you want... the whole experience."

She glanced at him and enjoyed the flush on his cheeks.

He groaned, thrusting into her. *Guess seeing my mouth full of his cock changed his mind.* He wrapped his hand around her head and pushed.

She allowed him for about a second. But it was her fling, and she wanted some, too, before he finished. She pulled back, letting go of him with a *pop*. His eyes glowed dark and wanton.

She grinned, rolling on the bed, away from him and onto her back. With a quick wiggle, she removed her pants. Bravado prevailed tonight. "My turn."

Man... conservative, sheltered Josephine demanding to be serviced by the building handyman... She crooked a finger at him, loving her own audacity.

He obliged, with a vengeance. He crawled onto the bed and pushed her legs apart. Probably taking a page from her book, he dove in with gusto and little prep. The boldness of it put her on the edge in seconds—really on the edge, not the fake "I *think* I'm having an orgasm" like every time before.

It was a heart-stopping, full-body, brain-exploding experience. Josephine let out a scream and then a resounding moan that went on forever. Her brain soared with delight and her body tingled everywhere. She flopped on the mattress, spent.

Brett chuckled, listening to Jo go on and on as she came. There was nothing like a woman who wasn't afraid to express herself. Her body was perfect, her face divine, but the unbridled way she'd come at his touch got him harder still.

He snagged the condom from the nightstand. With infinite care, he rolled the latex on, while Jo writhed on the bed in pure bliss.

Nice.

He didn't always have such an effect on women, but sometimes things clicked. And tonight things clicked all over. He touched her leg to attract her attention.

She seemed to swim up from a dream. "Yeah?" she asked, her voice heavy and thick.

"You ready? Still wanna..." He held out a hand, not wanting to say more, but consent was a must.

She didn't answer, merely pressed her body against his and kissed him. Full, luscious lips pressed against his for several seconds before they parted.

Brett had kissed many women in his thirty-four years, but never like this. The kiss was deep, connected, and soul-sucking. He could kiss her forever. And not some high school make-out session, but a truly connected act between two adults. When she broke away, he mourned the loss of her lips.

"Yes, Brett," she said, breathy, sexy, and demanding. Their lips met again as they folded onto the bed, their bodies entwined.

He wanted her, wanted to pound her into the mattress with a Tarzan yell, but more than that, he wanted to kiss her till dawn. But the ache in his balls, the demand of his body became too much. He slid his kisses sideways to her jaw, her neck.

"Ready?" He almost couldn't form the words. In response, she wrapped her legs around his back. He entered her in one stroke. His brain sizzled, and his skin fried as her body closed around him. He forced himself to slow way the hell down before he came immediately.

They both lay motionless for a good minute, kissing while connected. Then his body kicked into overdrive. He moved with the speed and endurance of an eighteen-year-old.

And she went with him, every move, every thrust. The woman was a goddess. And when she came again, with another scream and a tight squeeze, he fell into bliss with her.

Josephine loved the sounds Brett made as he came, manly grunts and quiet curses. None of the pathetic excuses of what's-his-name or the whimpers and tears of Dexter.

All man.

He collapsed over her, but not on her, resting his head on her stomach, his warm breath coming in pants across her skin.

She could get used to this.

Gently, he rolled away, leaving her puddled in the center of the beautiful bed. Her mind floated in the bliss. Only one thought broke through—*so much better than a stupid ski weekend*. A handsome man, who treated her like a real person. She curled into him, loving the feel of his body against hers. Never in her wildest dreams would she have imagined taking the man to her room. Well, in her *wildest* dreams...

She giggled.

"What's so funny?" he asked.

God, she wanted to roll up in his deep voice and stay there for a week. Inviting him to the room seemed bold and reckless, and the best decision she'd made in a long time. Life was good.

"Oh, nothing," she answered, turning on her side. "This is a pleasant way to spend a Friday afternoon." She reached over and dragged her fingers down the taut, hard muscles of his back. *Mmm, round two might be in sight.*

She blinked, letting flashbacks roll through her mind. Part of her wanted this to be the start of something. Maybe she'd blow off the party and curl up with Brett for a few days. A grin spread across her face. It was exactly what she wanted.

"Hey, Brett..."

The lock of her door rattled, and Jo sat up with a gasp. Someone breaking into the room? Thank God Brett was here.

He glanced at her, and she whined low, her eyes about to pop out of their sockets. He laid a finger on his lips and stood, snagging his jockeys on the way.

Snatching the sheet, Jo pulled the covers to her neck as the lock rattled again.

Brett crossed the room. At the door, he dipped into his tool belt, snagging a hammer.

Jo gulped. Fear filled her gut. *Who would have the audacity to break into a hotel suite in the middle of the day?*

Brett twisted the bolt lock and wrenched the door open. His broad back covered most of the doorway, blocking Jo's view. In a deep voice, he asked, "Can I help you?" He sounded so intimidating and manly, she would have swooned if fear hadn't clutched her heart.

A familiar voice sounded from outside. "Who are you?"

Chapter Eleven

Jo scrambled from the bed, wrapping the sheet around her toga-style. She flew to Brett, grabbing his arm. With a tug, she forced him to lower the hammer. Then she turned to the would-be intruder.

Erica Lockwood, her mother.

"Mom..." she said, letting her disappointment fill her words.

Erica sucked in a breath, her hand at her throat. "What are you doing in my room, you beast?" She swatted at him with her purse, pushing her way into the suite. "And where are your clothes? You foul..."

Jo cut her off. "Mother!" She stepped in front of Brett, who looked ready to raise the hammer again. "What are you doing here? Were you trying to get into *my* room?"

"My room," she corrected with an air of shock. "I paid for it, Josephine. Therefore it is my room, child. Now, what is *he* doing here?" When she reached the couch, she spun dramatically. Her eyes darted from Brett to the walls to the furniture to Jo, her nose wrinkling.

Jo read her mind. *Good, but not good enough.* Never good enough. Nothing was—not the beautiful antiques, the rich decor, or Josephine.

When their eyes met, her mother's face twitched in disgust. "Where are *your* clothes, my daughter?"

Jo sighed, ready to close the door when a cough stopped her. Dexter Charlton stood in the doorframe, his lips pursed as usual.

Dear Lord in heaven. She brought Dexter. The weekend just went from bad to worse.

"Come in, Dexter." Jo waved him in, too polite to let the dweeb hover in the hallway. He smiled, flashing his buck teeth, and shuffled into the room. The door closed behind him, slamming shut like a jail cell.

"Mom..." she began, ready to argue about being an adult, and privacy, and...

Her mother cut her off. "Get your clothes on, young lady. And you"—she pointed at Brett—"need to leave my room."

A bolt of frustration and anger exploded inside her. Her room, her moment with Brett, her life, her chance... A boldness rolled over her. She refused to lose Brett because of her mother.

"No, Mom, you get out."

Mother blinked, taken aback. Dexter raised his eyebrows, the first movement from him.

Brett smirked. "Want me to throw her out?"

Jo smiled at him, already in love. Finally, someone who cared about her wishes. But she wouldn't subject the man to her mother if she could help it. Not when it was so new.

With resignation, she said to Brett, "No. Why don't you get dressed and head downstairs? I'll deal with this."

His twisted lips said, *not impressed.*

"I think I'll wait," he replied, crossing his arms over his bare chest. And the hammer still rested in his hand. Her very own Norse god.

Damn.

Mom screwed up her face, her anxiety plainly displayed. "Please, young man"—her tone teetered on the verge of pathetic—"This is none of your concern. Get dressed and leave immediately, or I'll call security." Her lips tight, she fidgeted her fingers, lacing and unlacing them.

Dexter stood like a statue, saying nothing.

Brett laughed. A beautiful, sexy sound.

Mom and Dexter needed to go now because Jo wanted to reward Brett immediately.

"Ma'am," Brett said politely. "You and your son"—Jo giggled, and Mom scoffed. Brett narrowed his eyebrows but continued—"need to leave. We know who rented the room."

He crossed to the door and opened it. As he passed Dexter, he placed an arm on the man's shoulder, ushering him to the exit. "If you wanna talk to Jo, I'm sure she'll be happy to talk with you in the lobby." He held out a hand for Erica, who ignored it.

Worry colored Erica's entire body, but her mouth stayed closed in a tight, lemon-sucking scowl. And miracle of miracles, the woman walked out without another word.

Once outside, she said with a sliver of disquiet, "Come to my room as soon as you're dressed. We will discuss this..."

Brett shut the door and snapped the lock.

He turned, his hands on his hips. "Okay." He stooped to pick up his clothes.

The burn of embarrassment consumed Jo. "I'm so sorry, Brett. She's... well..." She waved a hand at the door. "A little overprotective. A lot overprotective. I'm sorry if she made you feel..."

He smiled as he put on his clothes, but he left the shirt open. "Like the hired help? It's not the first time I've been caught with my pants down. Don't worry." He paused, his lip caught in his teeth for a moment. "I didn't like the way she talked to you."

His gaze searched the room. He looked everywhere but at her, as if he wanted to say more. Instead, he shrugged. "I'll get out of your hair, so you can deal with that." He waved a hand at the door, his bare chest distracting her thoughts.

Jo bit her lip, not wanting Mom's intrusion to end what might have been days of bliss. "Again, I'm sorry, Brett. She's very controlling, and I... well, I've been asserting my independence, and she doesn't like it. She's upset. I didn't mean to mix you up in..."

He held up a hand, stopping her babble. "Not mixed up. No worries." He said the words lightly, but they stung deeper than she expected. The whole thing rushed by too fast. She wasn't ready for it to be over.

She ran a trembling hand over her forehead before meeting his gaze again. As their eyes locked, she remembered her place. "Again, I'm sorry, Brett. Thank you for..." Awkwardness fell over her like a blanket. She walked toward him, her hand held out for a shake.

He grabbed it and pulled her close, pressing her sheet-wrapped body to his bare chest. He paused for a millisecond, then kissed her, one of those deep, soul-sucking kisses he'd been laying on her all afternoon. Her toes curled into the carpet.

As he broke the kiss, he put a knuckle under her chin. "If you're staying the weekend in her room..." The word "her" dripped with sarcasm, and she smiled. "I'll be around working on the west wing. The balcony door might stick again." He winked.

Grabbing his tool belt, he flipped the lock and headed into the hall. The click of the door shutting echoed through the room.

He was gone.

She stood staring for a few seconds, willing him to come back. Hadn't they just shared something wonderful? Too wonderful for him to leave so quickly?

Her heart sank.

She sat on the bed, a myriad of emotions running over her. Confusion and anger blurred her thoughts, and nothing seemed real. Tears stung at her eyes, both for Brett's leaving and for her mother's behavior. But one thought prevailed: *Prince Charming has left the building*.

Once she composed herself, Jo dressed in a rush, grabbed her key card, and headed out the door. Who should she go after first? Brett, to apologize, or Mom, to teach her some lessons about privacy? Conflicted, she lingered by the elevator.

"In here, Josephine." Her mother's voice rang in the hallway.

Jo's shoulder rose to her ears, and her mouth turned into a grimace. A wave of embarrassment and trepidation rolled over her. The conversation with Brett would have to wait. Mom, as always, came first. Jo spun on her heel and marched toward the open door just down from her room.

Erica stood there, silhouetted in the doorway, her chin high, her eyes narrowed.

Jo wanted to smack that chin, but what could she do? Her mother had sacrificed so much over the years. The least Jo could do was be a dutiful daughter. Slapping your mother, no matter how she embarrassed you, was never a suitable option.

Head down, she shuffled past her mother into the room. It mirrored her own, with less acreage. The bed sat to one side, an overstuffed couch on the other. She threw herself on the seat, wondering how to have this conversation.

Her mom took her time closing the door and locking it. At length, she crossed the room and sat daintily on the bed. After what felt like six hours, she looked up at Jo. Her expression held disappointment and sorrow.

Jo sighed, plunging in rather than waiting for the reprimand. "Mom, he's..."

Her mother's hand flashed up in a millisecond. "I don't want to hear anything about that man. I've let you down. I should've driven up with you and shared the room. I never dreamed..." She let the words taper off, her hand pressing into her chest.

Conflicting emotions battled inside Jo. Part of her wanted to laugh at her mother and tell her off. Jo could sleep with whoever she wanted. But the other half of her felt the shame and embarrassment of being literally caught with her pants down.

And this woman who'd cared for her through twenty-plus years of childhood illness. How could she be angry or mean to her? She meant well, wanting to take care of Jo. Guilt crushed her like a bug.

"Mom, I..." God, what could she say? Sorry? But she wasn't. And at her age, she shouldn't have to explain herself or her sex life. "We met, and we..."

"We have a dinner tonight with Dexter, his family, and several other guests. I've arranged for a private dining room. I hope you brought something appropriate to wear."

And that was the end of that talk.

Jo sunk into the couch. Her mother was a force of nature, and there was no moving her off course once she set her mind to something.

Jo tried anyway. "He's nice, and he's..."

Her mother stood and wandered to the door of her balcony. Jo almost warned her about loose handles but closed her mouth.

"You have thirty minutes to get ready. I'll meet you in the lobby." With her back still to Jo, she crossed her arms and raised her chin again. A dismissal.

Jo raised herself from the couch. She should blast her mother and tell her what a nice guy Brett was. Otherwise, she could ignore her mom and blow off the dinner. But she wouldn't. The guilt would eat her alive.

Yes, she had submitted her game and was almost free to go, but the weekend... It would be their last big holiday party. The last of a tradition that began when Father passed. He'd been gone for over twenty years. Time to move on, but for one more night with the two of them surrounded by friends. How could she deny her mother just a few more days before she flew the coop?

Brett hesitated before hitting the dining room for supper. He hadn't heard from Jo since he'd left her room. Of course, she didn't have his number. But the front desk would tell her how to get ahold of him, wouldn't they?

Guilt tied his stomach in loopy knots. It wasn't the first time a parent had shooed him out of their kid's room, but this time seemed different. He didn't know Jo's exact age, but she wasn't some kid. And he was not taking advantage of her. The whole situation was mutual.

So, why hadn't he called her a few hours later to check on her? *Because I'm a dumbass*. More regret stirred inside him. It was kinda her call. But...

This was not how things worked in his universe. Normally, her mother storming in would be an understandable end to the affair. But Jo lingered in his thoughts, almost blinding him with feelings, ideas, and daydreams. It all seemed so different, so new.

In the dining room, he noticed a barrier set up on the far side. The Excelsior didn't have those modern sliding walls like most hotels, because of the weird tiered-seating arrangements. (The room needed a complete overhaul, but that was an argument for another day.) From his guesstimate, about twenty people sat behind the makeshift wall for a private meal. Through a space in the panels, he could see his Jo at the head table.

Something in his chest clunked. Every inch of him wanted to run over to her, scoop her up, and carry her off like some fairytale princess, despite her mother sitting right there next to her. The woman looked like she'd been sucking lemons.

Jo looked defeated. Her head hung low, and she nibbled at her food. How could she be the same woman who gobbled down the salmon last night?

Frozen in the dining hall entrance, he watched her, willing her to pick up her head and see him. If only those gray eyes would lift and he could bask in her smile. He waited. She never looked up.

"Hey, Brett," Javier said, "Your table's set. Let's get you out of the line of traffic."

Chapter Twelve

Jo woke the next morning with mortification still looming over her. She paced the room, considering what to do next. Her mom brought Dexter as Jo's beau-de-jour. Dinner had proven that. Mom forced her to sit next to Dexter throughout the meal, while hints of after-dinner "activities" were thrown at her.

Eww.

Been there, done that. No thank you on seconds.

She collapsed onto the bed, her emotions racing between anger with her mother and the bliss of being with Brett. Sex with him changed her whole view of the universe. Never before had it been as wild, raw, and exciting. For the first time, she wanted as much for him as for her. It sounded super selfish, but usually, sex focused on the man and not her. Usually, the guy left her wanting more.

But Brett took care of her, wanted her happy and satisfied. She must return the favor. Perhaps that was what an actual relationship was like—real sex, authentic emotions—no one trying to get one over on the other before crawling away and not returning phone calls.

An image of Dexter rose in her mind. Meek and nerdy around Mom, condescending and snobbish as soon as she disappeared. What would he think of big, tough, blue-collar Brett?

Giggling, she rolled around on the still-unmade bed. She didn't care what Dexter thought. Not a snip. Nor did she care what her mom's impression was. Brett was exactly what she needed.

Damn, why hadn't she gotten his number? She should call and ask him to the party. Yes, Mom tossed him out like the unwanted help. When did he say he was leaving? She couldn't remember.

Snatching the phone, she dialed the desk. When the clerk answered, she requested Brett's room number and for the call to be transferred. And of course, with her luck, one of the giggly clerks answered.

"Do you have a problem in your room again, Miss Lockwood?" Her tone sounded snide and condescending. Jo bristled. "I can send Ernie any time."

Jo was tired of games, tired of people acting like she was a bubble-wrapped princess, tired of this bitch treating her and Brett like the town joke. Seriously, why? And she must have been mad, because she'd never called another person a bitch, not even in her mind.

Ever.

"Please connect me, or give me his cell number." She kept her tone flat, confident. Usually, she asked with a whiny, begging voice. The tone always worked on Mom. The more pathetic, the more Mom gave her.

But it stopped now.

Her computer game was submitted, with all the accompanying paperwork. She'd met a fantastic new man. Together, they'd solved a hotel-wide cable problem. Once she got the job and started getting regular paychecks, she'd find an apartment and start her brand-new life.

The clerk, Tiffany, she thought, huffed and hummed. "Let me ask the manager."

"No," Jo cut her off. "Don't bother." She slammed the phone down, prepping to deliver a scathing report to the management about the mistreatment. Halfway to the door, she stopped.

Mom would do that. And coming from Jo, it might appear to be a juvenile tirade. A spoiled brat begging her due.

Jo didn't want to be that girl. She didn't want to be like her mom, didn't want to use her name, her condition to demand things. Grabbing her keycard, she headed downstairs to find Brett herself.

Brett stood back from the last toilet he needed to install. He rechecked everything, hoping for no leaks in his haste. The adrenaline from the afternoon fueled a work frenzy—new pipes installed, and the shower wraps done. He should have been using the extra energy with Jo, except her over-protective, vindictive mom had interfered.

So, he vanished to the west wing to finish his job. He hurried, in case Stanley showed and chastised him for slacking on the job. Brett put his nose to the grindstone, even working over the weekend. And he hadn't taken off when Ted called about Dad's bad decision. He still didn't have all the data about the business situation at home and probably needed to return soon.

He glanced around the bathroom. A few more hours to complete the last room, then he'd go home without the guilt of shorting Stanley a day. If the job was done, it was done. And he'd even helped Jo restore the internet, so...

And of course, Stanley knocked on the door. "Got a minute?" he asked, poking his head into the room.

Brett's shoulders fell, knowing what Stanley had to say.

"It's about the Lockwoods." His tone sounded resigned, almost apologetic.

"Let me guess," Brett said, heaving himself from the floor. "I must stay away from Miss Lockwood. I'm not allowed to be in the room with her. Mrs. Lockwood will have my head if I go anywhere near her daughter."

Stanley cracked a grin. "Pretty much. Gotten the speech before?"

"Too many times." Brett hit the handle on the new toilet, and miracle of miracles, nothing overflowed, backed up, or leaked. "It's the first time the lecture's pissed me off." He turned on the faucets of the sink, letting the taps flow. Again, things worked. Hot flowed out of the correct side. He'd finished the shower earlier. He washed his hands, his back to Stanley. In the mirror, their gazes caught.

"Big client, and..." Stanley held his hands out in a "what can you do" gesture.

"And I'm pretty sure her little darling is not only over eighteen but tipping toward thirty. I won't spout about how the woman has no right to dictate Jo's life. Nor am I going to piss and moan about how Jo blew me off." He wiped his hand on a towel.

Stanley laughed. "Blew? Interesting verb choice." He grinned.

"I broke the rules, but she came after me." Guilt hit him. "No, it was mutual. We both wanted it. I don't care what her mother claims. She's an adult, with an adult brain. So..." He furrowed his brow, confused by the rationalization. He didn't need to explain to Stan.

"Are you almost done with the repairs?"

Brett nodded.

"Finish and head out. I won't interfere in your love life, but knowing your reputation..."

"You tell her that?" He turned, his hands on his hips, well aware of how he towered over Stanley. "Because it'd be a shitty thing to do. I'm not some kid..."

Stanley held up a hand. "I didn't say anything to the mother or the girl. I told her you'd be scarce for the rest of the weekend." He raised his eyebrows as if seeking consent.

"Fine," Brett said. "But, like I said, she's an adult capable of making her own decisions."

Stanley sighed, crossing his arms. "Please try to keep it in your pants. You know what the deal is, right?" The vibes coming off him seemed ugly and harsh. It wasn't as if Brett had attacked the woman, or that she was underage.

"Yeah, the controlling mom forced her to go to a party..."

Stanley swallowed. "Wedding," he said the word with a squeak.

"Okay, wedding... and she got here early to work on her computer project..."

Stanley cleared his throat, stopping Brett's speech. "Her wedding."

Brett's eyebrows popped up. "The mom? She didn't tell..."

Stanley put a hand on Brett's arm. His eyes brimmed with sympathy. "Josephine's wedding. The staff was told to keep quiet. According to the mother, Jo wanted everything to be on the downlow. No big fanfare. Just go along with the party thing."

Brett stared at him, his mouth agape.

Jo is getting married?

Jo was getting married today and didn't bother to mention it once. She slept with him but planned to marry some other dude in a couple hours. He was her bachelorette party.

"Fuck." Brett spun away from Stanley, placing his hands on the sink. Fire and fury boiled under his skin.

Jo—sweet little shy Jo, computer programmer, fixer of Wi-Fi *fucking lied* the whole time. Another high-society predator like her mother, who wanted him for a last fling before being tied down. Hell, she probably planned the rescue from the balcony thing.

She used him.

His stomach churned, sick with anger. He'd charge into that wedding... he'd... do nothing of the sort. Not if he wanted further business with these bluebloods. He was a tool for the high classes to play with, and he had been played well.

"Fuck!" He screamed the word this time. Clutching the sides of the sink, he shoved his anger into the innocent object and heaved. The pedestal sink tore from the wall, ripping pipes and the sheetrock. He tossed it to the floor, uncaring about the spraying water or shattering porcelain.

He brushed past Stanley, who stood stock-still, his eyes open wide. "Bill me."

Josephine walked through the confusing corridors of the Excelsior until she found the oldest wing. The dated wallpaper and threadbare carpet validated the hotel owner's decision to renovate. But the bones seemed fine. Brett's company could spend the entire winter here fixing the rooms. And in the spring, the hotel would have another wing full of customers.

Brett said he'd finish the job today. Hopefully, he hadn't left yet. After the scene with her mom, she desperately wanted to talk to him, to explain, to see if any spark remained between them.

She paused halfway down the hall, a sinking feeling coming over her. The dark stretch of hall spoke of horror movies and jump scares.

Jo wasn't an adventurous person by nature, and the wild, willy-nilly search for Brett seemed impetuous. She hunched a little, ready to call it quits, when a door two rooms down burst open, and Brett charged out.

He looked like a pissed-off bull, his cheeks red, his fists at his side, his face scrunched in deep emotion. A squeak escaped Jo's lips as she flattened to the wall, out of his path. His gaze met hers, and the anger didn't dissipate.

Uh-oh.

They stood there, feet apart, staring hard at each other. Brett caved first.

He pulled himself up to his full height, his gaze still boring down on her. "Speak of the devil," he muttered.

Jo did not understand how to react to that. *What did that mean?* She glared at him, waiting for clarification. Yes, she erred, mostly because of her mother's behavior, but his anger seemed over the top. "I'm glad I found you."

"Oh?" he asked, as he crossed his arms. Apologies wouldn't work here if his feelings ran that deep. But she had to try. She didn't want to lose him because of her mother's snobbish attitude. The truth of the thought gave her the strength to step forward.

"I wanted to apologize for..."

Brett waved her words away before she began. "Busy here. I gotta work for a living. Busted pipe needs fixing."

Stanley poked his head out of the room Brett had exited. "You will fix this, right?" he asked. The man seemed skittish and worried. His gaze met Jo's, and his eyes widened, but he said no more.

Brett spun, the heat of his anger radiating far enough for Jo to sense it on her skin. "Of course, I'll fix it. That's my job, right? Mopping up messes. Fixing things so everyone can have an easy day in your pretty hotel." He turned again, heading toward her. "I need a pipe wrench," he muttered.

He didn't glance at her as he passed. She raised a hand to touch his arm, but his violent expression gave her pause. Not the time to invite him to the party, to apologize for Mom, to pursue the relationship she so desperately wanted.

Her heart squeezed. Had she lost him before they began? If her mother had anything to do with this, she'd give her an earful.

She hurried down the hall in Brett's wake, ignoring Stanley as he called for her. *Another of Mom's flunkies.* That was done and over. She'd promised to attend the party, but afterward, she'd find her own life without smarmy men like Stanley, and definitely without her overbearing mother. The women's shelter had plenty of room if she needed it. Maybe the family lawyer could give her some of the tiny trust fund from Father, even though she couldn't touch it until her thirtieth birthday.

It didn't matter.

If Mom chased Brett away, she'd jettison every other nice man who entered her life. Jo was tired of being her mother's doll, of being coddled and pampered. She was entitled to a life better than this.

"Brett," she called as she reached the lobby door. He stopped, but his shoulders were at his ears. "I want to apologize for my mother." He didn't turn, so she continued. "It's hard to understand the dynamic of my family." The muscles in his neck tightened further. "But she doesn't speak for me. Please understand."

Brett had enough. He liked Jo—a lot, but the poor-little-sick-girl thing got old super-fast. She'd become a different person once her mother arrived. All the boldness drained out of her. She became a meek and mild wuss, instead of the quirky, strong woman he'd slept with.

When she asked for understanding, something broke inside him. She'd never be free of her mother. She'd always be Mommy's little girl and not the woman he needed. He mourned for losing the goddess who'd invited him into her bed yesterday.

His temper escaped. "Do you understand your ma has you under her thumb? She dictates your life because you're a little"—he waved his hands at her body—"fragile. You're not a child, but you let her baby you." He wanted to mention her impending wedding, to throw it in her face, but something in him wouldn't allow it.

She must have known. It was her goddamned wedding. Women attended dress fittings, parties, and planning sessions. Jo had slept with him as a last rodeo before marrying that cardboard cutout who came to her room. She'd never have the passion with Dexter that they'd shared.

And that was a damned fact.

"It's complicated, Brett. My illnesses and my mother..." Her chin fell to her chest as if the word "mother" explained it all.

"It's not. You can't eat wheat. You know it. She knows it. You built an entire world in your computer..." He stopped as the epiphany hit him. The computer game represented an escape, a virtual world away from the mother. No wonder she liked computers. She could jump online and escape anytime.

"And what?" Red crept into Jo's cheeks. Her hands fisted at her sides, and her mouth drew into a straight line. She was finally pissed, too.

Good.

"And..." Images of the wedding, of Jo's potential future, of a situation he couldn't fix with his tools flooded his brain. "And someday, when you finally get the guts to stand up to your ma, come find me. Right now, I gotta fix a busted pipe." Without another word, he headed to Ernie's tool room/server room/ mancave. He'd make the guy help him repair the damage so he could take off today. He didn't want to be here when Josephine Lockwood strolled down the aisle.

Chapter Thirteen

Josephine walked into her room in a daze. Brett's words bored into her core. Inside, her heart felt damaged, bleeding, her brain addled. He had a point, and part of her could not admit it. She'd been under Mom's thumb her entire life—sickness or no.

Now that she had a diagnosis and traveled the road to a healthy life, why wasn't she living it? Why stay here in the hotel rather than get her own apartment? Why did she come at all? If she stayed home, she might have turned in the audition program earlier. Why hadn't she told her mother about the game?

Why hide?

Blinking back tears, she shuffled into her suite like a zombie. Of course, her mother was there, with her complete access to Jo's private room, and all other aspects of her life.

Jo wiped at her eyes, ignoring her mother's greeting. She staggered to the bathroom for a long, hot soak, and then she'd check out of the damned hotel.

She turned on the taps, her mind wandering to Brett's statement about fixing pipes. An excuse to avoid her.

Probably. After yesterday, who could blame him?

Splashing the water to check the temp, she considered leaving immediately. Forget the pampering and head out the door. She'd have to use the credit card Mom paid for until she had her own card. And honestly, as long as the laptop traveled with her and internet remained available, she'd earn a living.

The idea of leaving didn't quite spur her to action yet, but it rolled around in her brain. She undressed. As she eased herself into the vat of bubbles, a rapid knock sounded on the bathroom door. Couldn't the woman leave her alone when she was in the tub? The handle rattled.

Apparently not.

"Josephine." Mom opened the door and scanned the room. "You need to get ready. Where have you been?" She sounded as if she were speaking to a child.

Jo finally heard it. She sighed, slipping deeper into the foam.

"The party begins in an hour," her mother said. "The hairdresser will be here in twenty minutes. Be ready."

"Mom," Jo said, lifting her chin from the water. "I'm not up to it. Can't I make an appearance and go home?"

"Josephine, you promised." Mom used her best guilt-inspiring voice. "Everything has been planned and paid for. I have so many social and business contacts arriving for it. My daughter cannot be absent. How would it look?" She sat at the edge of the tub, skimming her hand on the water. "I'm aware that man..." She refused to meet Jo's gaze. "But perhaps another time you can speak to him and clear up what happened. We have an obligation tonight. After that..."

Jo studied her mom as she stared at the floor. An air of enigma surrounded her. She was usually the queen of passive-aggressive, but tonight she seemed subdued. Did she still demand Jo attend, or was there something more?

Sitting up straighter, she touched her mother's hand. "Want to tell me what's really going on?"

Her mother stood, spinning away. "It's the usual guest list, but you need to make connections. Your health is better, but I won't always be here to ensure you meet the right people. If you connect with these families tonight, I'll feel better about your situation when I'm gone."

"Situation?" Jo asked, exiting the tub. "You're sixty-two. Is there something you're not telling me?"

"I'm fine," she said, examining her chin in the mirror. "I'm merely concerned about you."

Jo snatched a towel from the rack. "I'm an adult. I can take care of myself."

"Oh, Josephine, we both know it isn't true. Your dietary issues are overwhelming. I can't tell you what I endured so you'd be safe at meals here. And the complications from your disease over time... Dr. Miller spoke about so many long-lasting problems. I..."

"Celiac is not a death sentence. In fact, it's a good time to have it because the general population is aware. So back off, Mom. Stop smothering me."

"Smothering, darling? I only want the best for you. You'll come tonight? For me?" And she chose that moment to spin around again, her hand clutched to her pearls, her eyes brimming with tears.

And the tears always got to Jo. The guilt, the pain, the *you're my only child* nonsense.

Jo sighed. "I didn't bring anything fancy to wear." She'd purposely brought basic clothing, hoping to opt out due to lack of formal wear.

"I have the perfect dress for you," Mom said.

Of course she did.

Brett glared at his phone. He didn't need this today. He'd fixed the busted pipe, cleaned up the mess, and lost the woman of his dreams. Another call from his brother was not top on his list.

Ted had left a cryptic voice mail, something about Ryan falling for the woman whose house burned down. Exactly what the Kramers needed, more suspicions their company was corrupt. First a sketchy fire, then Ryan being the inspector, next Ryan not being able to keep it in his pants. And he held the reins at Kramer and Sons.

Brett fumed.

Fucking Ryan.

He always skated out of these situations with his ass perfectly clean, while leaving his brothers to pick up the mess.

Like the mess in Albany. He didn't think his little brother had anything to do with the bribes and false reports, not straight-laced Ry. And he got out it without a smidge of dirt on him. And now he was the building inspector for Stonewater.

Brett never wanted such a job, but for Mayor Denise Anthony to not consider him or Ted was insulting. Two hometown boys who understood the business, who still lived there and added to the economy. Maybe he shouldn't have chased the woman's daughter.

Not that Ted helped much these days. He'd had trouble focusing and got mad in a heartbeat since Cheryl left a year ago. Everyone assumed there'd be a wedding last fall, but the woman disappeared one day—just left his brother hanging. Her family refused to even speak to Ted.

Brett sniffed around a bit, and the grandmother finally relented, saying Cheryl moved away to put her life in order. In other words, she dumped Ted so hard, she left the state.

Resigned to the mess, Brett called his brother back.

Ted answered in one ring. "Your fucking brother." The three of them always seemed to begin conversations that way. It was funny, but sad.

Brett saw their future as the old men at the general store, sitting together talking like best friends.

Maybe someday.

"Tell me the deal. Should I come home?" Brett cut to the chase, uninterested in listening to another recount of pompous Ryan, asshole Earl Porter, and stoic Dad. Brett knew it already.

"Nah, probably not. We talked, Ryan and I." Ted sounded resigned.

"So, we aren't at fault?" They'd installed the new lights, electrical, and a ventless fireplace. He also recalled how Earl did most of the renovations behind his wife (now ex-wife's) back. And Earl fired them.

Brett prayed the fire was accidental or had happened because Earl canned their butts in the middle of the job. Brett walked away. Ted fumed because he and Earl had kinda been friends. But some people never mature past their high school glory days. Earl certainly hadn't. He'd left Stonewater after the separation, and the town seemed lighter with him gone.

Ted broke through his thoughts. "Nope. Ryan and Dad had it all wrapped up in a few hours. Earl 'finished' the job and screwed up the electrical."

Brett sighed with relief. Ryan wouldn't lie if they were at fault.

When they were in school, Brett begged Ryan to do his homework so he, Brett, could still play football. Ryan refused, though he had great grades and tons of time to do extra work. Brett even offered to pay, but Ryan insisted it spelled cheating and refused.

Brett gave him wedgies for a week when the coach removed him from the team. Dad finally intervened on Ryan's side. But the pain of a super-wedge hadn't gotten his bro to lie.

Best/worst trait about his little bro, he was honest to a fault.

Brett sighed, and Ted mirrored the sound.

"I'm gonna help him fix up Ms. Porter's house. Least I can do at Christmas. Ryan's being all big man about it, too."

"Yeah, well, if she's his girl now..." Brett played mediator most of the time between the two. Ted hated how Ryan outshone him in every venue. Ted needed to get over his penis envy and live his own life. Someday he might see Ry's being a smart, arrogant boy scout wasn't bad.

"When you coming back?"

Brett considered. Stanley hinted perhaps Brett should take a break from the repairs until the Lockwoods left the building. He'd head out, and Ted would finish the job and keep the company name good.

"Guess I'll be back tonight. I gotta pack up."

"That was quick," Ted said. "I thought you were working on Stanley to have us to redo the entire wing."

"I was," Brett admitted, "But I screwed up today, and I'm taking a break."

"Fuck, we don't any more bad press, Brett. What did you do?"

Brett hated when Ted pulled the big-brother act—which he did, frequently. Ted always forgot there were only twelve months between them. And in their thirties, a year didn't account for shit.

"I had a problem. I fixed it. But Stanley got mad at me. I'm gonna come home for a few days, then see what he wants to do. No press, big bro. A misunderstanding on my part."

Ted huffed. He knew Brett too well, and Brett knew he knew it. "Whadja do?"

Brett chuckled. "Ripped a sink out of the wall."

"Isn't he paying you to do that?" Ted laughed, too.

"Yeah, not after I'd just fixed it and not with the water still hooked up." Before Ted revved up further into big brother mode, Brett plowed on. "I cleaned up the mess, repaired the damage, and told Stanley I'd pay for parts and service. Yes, a loss for the day, but I was civil, and hopefully he understands the situation."

Ted scoffed. "Woman?"

Rubbing his hand over his mouth, Brett admitted, "Yes, a woman, but not some random hookup like you're thinking. A nice girl I like, but she pulled a fast one. I got pissed."

"And you ripped a sink out of a wall. Glad to see some things don't change, bro." Ted snickered. "Come home, we'll grab a beer, then hunt down Ryan and give him a wedgie."

Brett didn't bother to argue. Ted signaled the conversation was over. He said good night and grabbed his suitcase. Good thing he traveled light. He wanted out of here and into his own bed more than anything.

After he finished packing, he glanced at his watch, wondering if he'd missed the fireworks of Jo's wedding.

Wedding. Fuck me.

Part of him wanted to stand at the door and wait for the *Does anyone here object?* part. He'd step forward and profess his undying love. When Jo looked confused and conflicted, he'd say, "Nah," and leave.

But he wasn't that much of an asshole, to screw with her whole life—not like her mother. He almost felt sorry for her. Maybe if she hadn't lied so well.

Josephine stood before the full-length mirror in her suite. She hated to admit the dress looked stunning, but it did. Her mother, for all her faults, her fussiness, her helicopter parenting, had great taste.

The simple, elegant, floor-length gown hugged every curve. And for once, Jo didn't mind a form-fitting dress. She'd put on a few pounds since she'd gotten her diagnosis. She had curves rather than bones to show off. The dress being backless didn't stop her from wearing it, either.

Such a dress meant the party was much more formal than Jo expected. The hairdresser arrived and put Jo's awkward brown mop into a tasteful chignon. The woman brought a thousand hair accessories to add to the bun, but Jo waved her off. She wasn't an ornamental girl. The dress said enough—long, classy, and white.

Usually, Jo avoided white dresses. Her pale skin and hair, combined with the fabric, turned her into a washed-out zombie, but the cut worked, and the crazy day added color to her cheeks.

She stepped away from the mirror, tired of playing dress-up. *Ten minutes at the party to schmooze and be nice to Mom's friends. Oh, and to placate Dexter, poor guy.* But Jo didn't think he'd be too disappointed in her turning him down. The man hadn't shown a lick of interest in her, and compared to Brett...

Jo let the thought pass. She'd blown it with Brett. Somehow, some way. Probably Mom pushed him away even more. But Jo had the idea she was to blame, and no idea why. He'd fumed over her dependence on her mother, and he was right. But to be so invested in it? They'd shared an intimate moment, yes, but...

Anyway.

She'd put herself out there to meet someone new. It almost worked.

A quick scan around the room told her nothing was missing. Her packed bags lay in a pile with her computer satchel on the top. Part of her wanted to bring it to the party, not let it out of her sight. But she'd uploaded the game to the cloud and sent the contracts to the company's lawyer. Now she must wait. The program was safe. She didn't have to lug it with her. But...

Once the party ended, she'd leave, head somewhere else for the rest of the weekend and leave Mom to her friends. Maybe she'd try the bed-and-breakfast Brett mentioned in Stonewater. She might see him, and...

Ugh, get off that train of thought! It was over. Brett didn't want her.

She grabbed her little clutch with her phone, credit card, and key in it. The front desk assured her baggage would be downstairs waiting for her.

Ten minutes.

Ten minutes and her entire world would change.

She'd be free of Mom. Her game was sold. She'd borrow money from the trust and finally start her life.

Jo paused at the ballroom doors. No one was in sight. Had she gotten the time wrong? She glanced at her watch.

Two pm.

Mom had been very clear about it. For a second, she considered finding Ernie the handyman's mancave, and playing a few rounds of an MMO.

No, I can do this. Mom asked nicely. With a deep breath, she opened the double doors, and all thought screeched to a halt.

Jo goggled at the scene. The room looked magnificent, decorated as a winter wonderland. Snowflakes sparkled from the ceiling. Dozens of tables were adorned with shimmering blue and white tablecloths, and pinecone centerpieces with white ribbons and roses.

Jo's hand went to her mouth. As a child, Mom never allowed her to play outside much. The cold and damp was always too much for her poor, sickly body. But the room personified the winter adventure she'd always wanted.

She focused straight ahead, hoping to find Mom and thank her for the lovely—

She stopped cold.

In front of the wall of windows with the beautiful New York snowscape stood an altar. Mom waited there, dressing in an elegant light blue damask dress. Next to her, Dexter fussed over his white tux with tails, dusting away imaginary lint. The guests formed an arc from the door to the altar, where a robed minister waited.

Jo's jaw dropped.

This looks like...

Chapter Fourteen

Music began to play. The first four notes of "Here Comes the Bride" were enough to shock Jo into reality. It was *not* a dinner party. *Mom had planned a wedding.*

A surprise wedding.

A wedding for Jo to a man she barely knew. How could... how did... why hadn't anyone clued her in?

She stepped back as the horror hit her, fighting back tears.

A wedding. Her beautiful white dress, and the hotel staff being so weird...

And Brett...

No wonder everyone snickered at them. They assumed he was her last liaison...

Guilt and anger flooded her veins. She swayed for a moment, staring daggers at the woman who gave birth to her, the woman who kept her hostage her entire life, the woman who humiliated her in front of these people.

Dexter stepped forward, holding his hand out, inviting her to walk down the aisle. Beside her, a figure appeared out of nowhere and handed her a bouquet.

Jo grasped the lovely bundle of roses and lilies. She glanced at it for a millisecond before hucking it as hard as possible at Dexter. The entire room froze as the flowers bounced off his chest and hit the floor.

"No fucking way," Jo screamed. She'd never spoken that word aloud before, but now...

She spun and raced to the front desk. "I want my..." At the same moment, a bell boy parked the cart with her luggage. She grabbed her computer bag. "I need a car." She told the clerk who looked at her bewildered.

"But Miss Lockwood, the party..."

Again, foul language took over. "Fuck that," she said and rushed out the door.

In the blowing snow, she turned left and right, unsure what to do. She spotted a truck parked near the portico, its back gate open. Jo hurried around to the passenger door.

"I need a ride," she called, hauling herself inside, dragging the tail of her dress in as she closed the door.

A man slowly tipped his head down to view inside the truck.

Brett.

"Sure, Jo. Where we going?" His voice sounded funny, cryptic, but she didn't care.

"Anywhere, Brett. Take me anywhere."

Brett tried about four times to say something. But each time he opened his mouth, the image of her in the dress, her hair all fancy, stopped him. She wore a wedding dress on her wedding day, and she sat in his pickup, driving away from the event as fast as possible—which, considering the blowing snow, wasn't so fast.

Finally, he glanced at her. "Did you do it?" he asked. His voice sounded tight, anxious.

Please say no.

Jo sucked in a breath as she pressed against her door. "You knew?" Her words were incredulous, accusing.

Oh, fuck. Maybe she didn't know about the wedding. No, she couldn't be that naïve.

"Did you?"

"No." She slapped her forehead. "Why did you... you know... with me if you knew I was getting married?"

Then again, maybe she was that naïve. "Sleep with you? Make love to you? Screw your brains out in the penthouse?"

"Brett!" she screeched and whacked at his arms. One of the blows landed hard and ripped his hand from the wheel. The car skidded to the right.

"Jo, be careful. I coulda crashed." He glanced at her.

Her hands curled against her chest, and she'd tucked herself into the corner of the seat, her knees to her chest, her eyes wide. A panic attack in the truck could be devastating.

"Okay, just breathe," he ordered, and their gazes met. She pulled in a huge breath, her cheeks coloring pink. "Big slow breaths, in and out. Get yourself under control. I'll drive slowly and keep us on the road. I do my job, you do yours."

She dipped her chin.

Brett stared at the pavement. Rural New Yorkers knew how to deal with foul weather. But it didn't mean the roads weren't filled with ski bunnies and snowboarders who couldn't drive in this weather. If he fixed his gaze on the way ahead, he didn't have to focus on the scared woman next to him. He needed to figure this out.

First, he wasn't driving her back to the Excelsior. Not tonight, anyway. Not under these conditions, and not with Jo freaking out. Second, he had to understand the situation between them. Never mind, he had a pile of shit waiting for him when he returned home. Tonight, living away from town proved to be a godsend. If he drove through Stonewater, he'd be tempted to stop at Ted's, or the shop, or grab a drink at the Brew House and shoot the shit, get the gossip. The business bullshit and the hysterical woman put a stop to the idea.

Third... what was third? Deal with Ryan? Dad? Ted? No. He chanced a look at Jo. Third entailed finding out what had happened here.

He still smarted from her lack of honesty, but seeing her reaction made him consider whether she'd lied at all. He glanced at her. She leaned on the door, her hand near her mouth. Tears rolled down her cheeks. Not the best time to demand the truth.

"Jo, did you...?" He needed to know, even if the answer was yes.

"No." Her voice sounded strained, upset. Her gaze met his. "I need to process..."

Brett nodded, his gaze on the road. Fifteen miles to home on backroads in snow. They'd be there in less than an hour. Time enough for soul searching.

Brett pulled into his driveway a while later. More like plowed into it. The snow had come down hard and fast, filling the space with six or more inches. With a sigh, he rested his head on the steering wheel. Jo'd have to stay with him tonight. He'd decided on the road, knowing that detouring to any town to find a hotel meant the expense of two rooms. No way was he staying in a room with her in a wedding dress. Shivers ran down his spine.

Women and weddings.

They were crazy for them. Every single girlfriend so far had whispered the W-word at least once in their relationship. And usually, uttering the word prompted him to break it off. He was not the marrying type. Not to short-sighted, brainless girls who only saw lace and diamonds. He'd never be a lace-and-diamonds kind of boyfriend.

Living in Upstate, he should be able to find hearty women who liked flannel and snowshoeing. But so far, he hadn't found one. He wanted someone to talk to, not just rock the bedroom. Someone with ambitions beyond being his arm candy. He'd never be a rich man working for his dad. Why couldn't women understand that?

He glanced over at Jo. The spotlight over his garage cast a bluish glow, like moonlight. The light pooled into the passenger side of the cab, bathing Jo. In her white dress, she looked like an angel come to earth. His breath caught in his chest. She was gorgeous, smart, and vulnerable.

Brett blinked a couple of times to erase the image of her princess-like pose, but it branded itself into his brain.

Without a word, he opened his car door, planning to sprint inside to toss cold water on his face. Hell, he should just bury his head in the snow. The light shining on her cemented his only real thought.

He loved her.

It hit Brett hard in the chest, as if someone had answered his wish. A smart, well-rounded woman with an excellent head on her shoulders. She had passions and faults, without being a sugar-daddy chaser.

He was just transportation here, nothing more, a means to escape from her mother and future husband. He paused, his heart sinking.

Husband.

The idea made his blood run cold.

Fuck.

Too bad she turned out to be off-limits.

He could do without this kind of crazy. Especially with all the crap from work. He wanted to talk to his dad, find out about Ryan, and return Ted to his old self. His family needed him. He didn't have time to rescue the princess—yet here he was.

Something snagged him as he exited the car. He turned to find Jo's hand gripping his arm. "Can you pull into the garage?" Her voice held some timidity, but something else lay beneath her words.

Fear?

Anger?

He blinked at her. Her mouth curled up into a pucker, her eyes hard. "I don't exactly have snow boots on."

He glanced at her feet, encased in delicate white shoes that looked too fancy to walk in, much less trudge up his driveway into the house. He sighed. "Stay there." As soon as the words left his mouth, he knew he'd regret this. An image of him carrying her inside in her wedding dress burned into his head. Like any other woman in her place, she'd see more to it than his helping her in the snow. And his wonderful Jo would morph into another one of those clingy women he dated, droning on about weddings and marriage.

But no going back now. He had to get her inside.

He hiked around the car, breathing deeply before opening her door. With no other choice, Brett opened it and scooped her out of her seat. Carefully balancing her in his arms, he walked the snowy path to his front door.

They stood together on the doorstep, Brett's cheeks burning, Jo shivering.

"Uh," she said, her body pressed against his. "Are you going to open the door?"

"The keys," he grumbled, "are in my pocket." The super-romantic gesture he envisioned of carrying her over the doorway in her wedding gown kinda flopped. He felt so stupid it hurt, but he was also relieved.

"Well, either I can try to reach them," she laughed, "or set me down and unlock it yourself. I trust you."

"If I put you down, the snow will ruin your shoes. That's why I carried you."

Jo examined her toes. "No, you carried me so that my sickly self kept her feet dry. Put me down, Brett. They're just shoes."

Wha...? Shoes not important? He'd never heard a woman utter those words before. He looked at her, gazing deep into her eyes, and something clicked in his heart and his head.

This woman.

No one else.

Only her.

Jo was the one.

He lowered her to the ground, leaving his arms wrapped around her. "Josephine..." he said, pulling her tight against him. He pressed his lips to hers, barely holding back the passion burning inside him. She resisted for about half a second before melting into him, giving herself up to his kiss.

Chapter Fifteen

Jo pulled away from the wild kiss. Her body trembled as she did—a shiver that had nothing to do with the cold.

Brett looked at her, his gaze filmed over with something she didn't understand. After a moment, the fog in his expression cleared.

"Oh shit, you gotta be freezing." He fumbled in his pocket, looking for those elusive keys.

And thank god for them. The idea of Brett carrying her into his house in the dress mortified her. It looked as if she'd dashed from one man to another.

And she ran from no one.

Well, except Mom. But the thing with Brett was so odd and new. At least it wasn't spoiled by some stupid, tropey romantic image. She'd stay with him for tonight, longer if the snow lasted. Maybe long enough to come up with an alternative life plan.

And the shoes? Who cared about them? They were not her wedding shoes, not by a long shot. The situation seeped into her brain slowly.

Her mother.

Planned a wedding for her.

To Dexter.

Without telling me.

Words failed her. *How could she do that to me?*

Brett unlocked the door and gestured for her to enter. He hadn't said a word since he stopped on the steps. Such a romantic notion to carry her into the house, but far away from where they were. Where did they stand anyway? Jo hadn't a moment to know the man beyond sleeping with him.

She hesitated, knowing she should go inside, warm up, and decide what to do. But going inside seemed like a statement. Some sort of commitment, declaration. *I'm not going there.* She would not run from one wedding into another serious relationship.

Brett stared down at her, his brow furrowed. He looked like he didn't know what to do, either. With a wan smile, she stepped over the threshold and into his world.

He followed right behind her with a preemptive, "Don't mind the mess. Uh, I wasn't expecting company. Ever."

"Hence the lack of holiday decorations?"

He shrugged, his cheeks pink. And not from the cold.

Such a telling statement. Brett appeared to be a lady's man with his amazing good looks, and that body—oof. But he'd been polite, kind, and respectful. A huge mark in his favor. But now, he seemed standoffish. Not because a stranger entered his house, but because of their connection. She glanced around.

Archways sat on either side of the small foyer with an L-shaped staircase in front of the main door. Two small hallways flanked the stairs. A couch stood on one end and a dining table on the other. Not a holiday decoration in sight.

A wry smile twisted her lips. She wondered if he entertained the brothers he mentioned.

The place was small with a sparse, manly decorative scheme of hunter green and dark woods. A chair rail split the foyer's walls, green on the bottom, and a rich textured plaster above. Jo touched the wall. The effect looked elegant without being overstated. It didn't seem Brett at all.

"Come on in the kitchen," he said, his words staccato. "Let me get you coffee or something."

She trotted behind him and asked, "How about a glass of wine?" A glass of chardonnay sounded perfect about now.

He chuckled. "That won't warm you up. Have a seat." He pulled out a chair from a small kitchen table. Wrought iron painted white, it sported flowers up and down the legs. Probably patio furniture. She put a hand over her mouth to stifle a giggle. Men left to decorate made interesting choices.

After fiddling with the coffee pot, he thumbed a finger down another little hall. "I'll grab you something to wear." He strangled on the last words, his cheeks flushing red. Ducking his head, he left the room in a rush.

In her patio chair, Jo opted to shuck the offending shoes. The dress needed to go, too, but standing naked in the kitchen would send Brett the wrong message.

Hopefully, he'd understand that. She never intended to use him to escape her mother. And she didn't sleep with him to break up the wedding.

After a minute, Brett returned carrying a few articles of clothing. He held up one in each hand. "You'll swim in these, but it'll get you through until we..." His words faded off as if he had nowhere to go.

She hadn't a clue, either. Anything could happen next. *Anything.*

"Uh, thanks." She stood, holding out a hand for the clothes.

He pointed behind him. "You can change in the laundry room, Uh, it's pretty clean. I hid the..." His cheeks blazed pink again. "Anyway, those have a drawstring, so..."

The awkwardness was killing her. Time to break it up.

"You have a laundry room off the kitchen? Oh, my God. That's awesome." She grinned and trotted to the closed door.

Brett laughed. "One of the reasons I picked up the place. I'm flipping it, in case you couldn't tell from the fancy stuff in the old place. Side project. Not part of Dad's business."

Jo came back to the kitchen, swamped in his t-shirt and sweatpants. The cinched drawstring barely held up the pants. "You flip houses, remodel hotels. What else?"

And she was genuinely interested. Her social contacts comprised lawyers, professors, and computer people. No blue-collar man was allowed to speak to her. Once in a while, she'd ask a gardener or a repairman to show her his work. Mom always shooed her away, citing her health, and the dangers of germs, working with her hands, and "those people."

And Brett, a likable guy with carpentry skills, who could probably build her a perfect desk for her computer. Something ergonomic—comfortable, durable, and handsome. Kinda like him.

He shrugged, pouring a couple of mugs of coffee. "This and that. My older brother is brilliant with drywall and carpentry. I'm good at renovations. Dad's the electrical guy, but he's retiring." He stopped talking as if making the coffee required all his attention.

"And there's one more brother, right? What does he do?"

Brett snorted. "He waltzes into town, and everyone goes gaga over him. Thinks himself some great managerial genius. Takes over the business, leaving me and Ted out in the cold."

"Oh, no." Jo never planned to open a can of worms, but discussing someone else's family problems sounded very distracting. And she needed a distraction. "That sounds terrible, and at this time of year..." She settled at the table and Brett handed over the coffee. She frowned at its lack of wine.

"Ryan's a pain in the ass. He's honest to a fault which might end Kramer and Sons, which would kill Dad. And Ted is so out of it..." His words faded off. "Look, I don't wanna burden you with my stupid shit. You're cold and had a crazy shock. I should help you." He shuffled his feet, still standing by the counter.

Jo tapped the chair next to her. "Listening to you makes me forget my overbearing mother and her nonsense."

Brett's chin hung to his chest, but his eyes glowed. He was probably dying of curiosity.

Laughing, she said, "Okay. Ask your questions. I'll be as honest as I can. But I'm telling you, if I get too pissed, I want my wine."

He laughed, shuffling over to the chair next to her. "No wine, just coffee. Sorry." Plopping into a chair, he set his coffee on the table. "You really didn't know about the wedding?"

"Did you?" She laughed. "I had no clue. I thought it was a holiday party. My nose has been stuck in my computer for months now. Mom planned my life around me, as usual. I've never gotten much input into what happens." She sipped the dark brew. "That's why the computer programing. I wanted to be independent. But she doesn't trust me on my own."

"So, she promised you to some guy like cattle? An arranged marriage? Your family does that?"

Jo laughed again, unrestrained. The idea of her mother using a cultural practice not her own...

Never.

"I have no idea what she was thinking. Other than she's always directed my life. Most of the time I felt too sick to care what she did. I let her organize things, take care of the problems, make everything easy. I missed so much. Now that I'm healthier, I can see the hole I dug myself into. And if the wedding wasn't the epitome of it."

She shook her head as tears threatened. She wasn't responsible for her mother's crazy notions. Mom probably assumed she'd never protest. Jo would have someone to take care of her, to cater to her health issues, pay for everything, and bulldoze every barrier.

But she didn't want that life anymore. She was tired of being treated as a child. She had a mind and wanted to use it—to explore the world and try to survive on her own.

Be free to fail.

She glanced at Brett, who raised his eyebrows. "Penny for your thoughts," he said, a slight smile on his lips.

"My mother is not an evil person."

He laughed, and Jo shook her head.

"If you had a kid who spent half her childhood in bed—sick, weak, tired, wasting away, you'd be overprotective, too."

Brett raised his coffee cup in salute. "Good to know. But you're better now?"

"Very much so. Apparently, that escaped my mother's notice. I never want to see her again."

Chapter Sixteen

Brett glanced at the beautiful woman at his table, buried in his sweats, in his house. Unbelievable. Rescuing her from her own wedding. *Jesus, could you get more soap opera?*

And now what should he do with her? He had his own problems to deal with. The stupid repairs at the hotel delayed, dealing with his family and the business. The repairs were almost complete at the Excelsior, and he needed to talk to Dad.

Brett glanced out the back slider, watching the snow fall. It could wait for tomorrow. He'd have to be out early with the plow, anyway. Many of his neighbors would be snowed in. He didn't want to think about them shoveling their driveways.

In this small town, everyone seemed too old to remove snow. No one flew south for the winter. They endured the weather, with neighbor helping neighbor. Plus, no way he'd let Dad shovel this heavy shit.

Jo cleared her throat, and Brett realized he'd asked her about herself, then slid into his own thoughts.

What a dick.

"Sorry," he chimed. "My brain automatically focused on the snow. You asked..."

Her cheeks reddened. "Oh, it's nothing. No biggie. Uh, so it's okay if I crash on your couch?"

Jesus, he was thick tonight. "Of course, of course. Stay as long as you want." The words popped out before he considered. Typical ingrained Upstate politeness. Dad taught him well, and now he had a house guest for a while. He didn't want to think about the girl's mother and the consequences when she found her daughter here.

He scrubbed the back of his neck. "Man, I might not have food you can eat. I don't want you to get sick." He glanced around his bachelor kitchen. Did he even have food in the fridge?

"If you have fruit and veggies, I'll be fine." She smiled, probably terrified she'd thrown her lot in with a mountain man. And now they were snowed in. In his mind, their intimate acquaintance helped. He'd have to feel her out about that. No pressure, especially after the wedding shit.

"Well," he considered. "I might have something in the fridge besides milk and juice. No bread, huh? I got eggs, I think. Anyway..."

She grinned. "Well, let's see what's for dinner." She rose from her chair, so cute in the oversized clothes. With her head in the refrigerator, she giggled. "Not as bad as I thought. Western omelets with bacon and fresh, uh, no fresh berries." Brandishing a basket of fuzzy blueberries, she grimaced. But her eyes twinkled with mirth.

"Yeah, about those..." He laughed. Her amused expression stopped his explanation cold. She didn't care, and his heart became lighter. He didn't have to explain away his failures. Ted would have teased, Ryan reprimanded, and Dad, well, Dad was no better than Brett.

All his life, he always overcompensated for the simplest mistake, overthought, blamed others, or demonstrated how he was not at fault. Jo, for some reason, eased the tension. He didn't have to talk about how he planned to make blueberry pancakes, but the call to go the Excelsior happened. And he forgot about them.

He didn't care. And it felt good.

Jo found the garbage and tossed the berry basket in. "Eggs and bacon it is. Wanna chop or cook?" She held up a green pepper. Her smile made his knees weak. For this woman, he might do both.

"Chop," he said, a dreamlike quality in his voice.

She giggled. "You into chopping? Is it a tool thing, Mr. Handyman?" She winked.

He pretended to be macho. "Yeah, give me those sharp tools and see what my manly hands can do." He stood, flexing his biceps. "I'll make mincemeat of those vegetables."

Laughter filled the room as they fell into the simple chore of making a meal. Brett marveled at the ease with which they chatted, cooked, and hung out. He could get used to it. Commitment didn't seem so scary around Jo.

Once they'd eaten with a nice light conversation weaving through the meal, Brett tipped back in his chair. He wanted to pull the woman into his lap and thank her properly for a fantastic meal. Well, eggs and bacon, but it seemed like an event.

Jo stood, taking his plate and hers. Without a conscious thought, he reached over and grabbed her hand to stop her from cleaning up. Sparks danced along their skin. Their gazes met, and the idea of lap-play drowned out most other thoughts. He held her delicate wrist in his hand. A minimal amount of effort would put her in his lap. Her gaze faltered for a second, and he let go.

The woman had run away from an awful situation. They'd made no promises after the first tryst. The last thing he wanted to do was pressure her into his bed, no matter how much he desired her. But he knew better than anyone, you can't always get the things you deserve, and he deserved her.

Instead, he offered her a smirk. "Guests don't do dishes, Jo. Go settle on the couch. I got this." He kept his words light, hoping his Upstate charm might hypnotize her into doing as he asked.

Her chin tucked to her chest. She didn't meet his gaze as she wove around him out of the kitchen. Once she'd passed him, he pointed out where the living room sat, sunk down a few steps. She said nothing as she passed into the room.

He swallowed hard, not sure what to make of that. Something transferred between them when their hands touched. But she'd been ordered around and pushed by her mom for so long.

Oh crap.

Did she think he did the dishes because he assumed she couldn't? Damn, walking on eggshells was tough, especially with someone he hardly knew. He never should've slept with her. It made everything a ball of tension.

He rounded up the dirty dishes and silverware. After a quick rinse, he tossed everything in the dishwasher. Tomorrow's chore. No point in using hot water on two plates and mugs. It gave him pause.

"You want more coffee or something?" he called into the living room.

She peeked around the corner. "If there's any left. It's kinda cold down here." As if to emphasize the point, she wrapped her arms around her chest and disappeared into the living room.

Fuck.

Did he touch the thermostat when they got home? He definitely hadn't started the woodstove. In the winter, he hunkered down in his favorite chair with the stove roaring out a good solid eighty degrees of heat. Without it, that room was like an icebox. And now, he had a guest, a tiny slip of a woman with zero body fat, and he'd never turned up the heat.

With a muttered curse, he reset the thermostat and headed into the living room. His brain already formed a thousand excuses for the lack of fire: she distracted him, they were hungry, he wasn't cold. He paused at the top of the small set of steps. He'd flaked, no biggie. Her teeth weren't chattering, and her skin had no bluish tint. *All good.*

"Sorry. I forgot to stoke the stove. I, uh..." He didn't want to throw an excuse, but regret twisted inside him.

"Oh, no worries." She smiled at him, wrapped in the quilt he left on the couch. Mom's ancient blanket kept him warm many nights in the howling winters. Jo looked perfect tucked into the corner, her feet underneath. He could get used to the image.

"I heat with..." He waved at the cast-iron stove in the fireplace. The incredible stupidity of the situation punched him in the gut. He focused on the firewood, kindling, and rolled paper instead of her. He should say something, talk about something. Do something. But the air hung with a strange energy, and he didn't know *what* to do now.

Once the fire hit a rolling pace, he closed the window door. Through the glass, a tiny fire flicked and danced, catching the larger pieces of wood. "Should warm up here pretty quick," he said.

He sat for a moment watching the flames, wondering if he should go set up the guest room for her. He'd have to clean the junk piled atop the bed. Or he could let her use his own bed. Also, the plow needed to be hooked up. Anxiety ate at his gut. If she weren't here, he'd do his usual thing. She distracted him.

He faced her, ready to decide—either take her upstairs or go outside to the truck.

The snow gods decided for him. The power cut out.

Chapter Seventeen

Worry fell over Jo in waves. More than just the snowstorm bothered her. She was alone with a handsome man, in the dark, in the cold. She'd slept with him, but she never dreamed she'd be on the run, in borrowed clothes. Now, she stood in the house of her rescuer. Did she owe him?

She watched as he lit a candle and a gas lantern. The room glowed with amber warmth. Chewing her lip, she glanced at the he-man standing over her with his lamp. His expression said it all. She owed him nothing. She didn't have to pay back the rescue, the meal, the place to stay with sex. A tingling sensation rushed over her. She couldn't remember the last time anyone treated her with respect like that.

Why wait?

He set the light down on the coffee table and rubbed his neck. "I should see if anyone needs a plow." His gaze rose to meet hers. His expression said he thought the same thing but didn't want to push. Such a gentleman. She opted to play the damsel in distress. It was a game she knew well.

"You're going to leave me alone in the dark?" She fluttered her eyelashes, awkwardness filling her gut. Did women still do that when seducing a man?

"Something in your eye?" he asked, his hand still scrubbing the back of his neck.

She stopped trying to flirt and spoke directly as she did at the hotel. "Brett, do you have to go out now? I mean, it might snow for hours, and then you'd have to plow again." She shrugged. How did she ask him to "plow" her? The idea made her giggle, and she ducked her face into the blanket.

"Uh," Brett hedged, perhaps reading her mind. "I, uh, don't have to, uh, now if..."

She stood, letting the quilt drop to the floor. "How about a tour of your house?"

Brett scratched his head. "In the dark?"

"Sure. Let's start with the bedroom." Amazed at her own brazenness, she grabbed his hand and tugged him toward the kitchen.

Scooping up the lamp, he let her lead.

Brett grinned as he showed Jo the upstairs. He played tour guide, but he wanted to toss her into his king-sized bed and play mountain man. She was nothing like he'd ever experienced before. He kept expecting her to be shy and reserved, even scared. But damn if she wasn't bold. Maybe it came from a life of entitlement, always getting what she wanted with a snap of her fingers. Well, anything but a life outside her mother's house.

The stupid wedding.

It was why she wasn't afraid to drag him upstairs. Or a way to get back at her mother. But Brett, the "love 'em and leave 'em king," sensed no malice from Jo. She wanted sex, so she asked for it. And sex with a guy of her choosing sounded more on the mark than revenge on her mom.

"And this is my room." He resisted throwing the door open in a huge fanfare. They both knew where they were headed.

Jo lingered in the doorway. "Wow, kinda masculine." She wasn't wrong. He'd gone with a navy-blue theme with oak wood, but seeing as he was over thirty and single, he could decorate as he damn well pleased.

She stepped into the room, seeming to hesitate, rethinking her bold move. Brett let her lead, though the idea of throwing her over his shoulder buzzed in his head.

"Pretty clean for a single guy." She'd stepped past him and glanced over her shoulder, mischief in her gaze. "I expected... well, I thought..." She blushed.

Actually blushed.

"Thought I was some kinda slob? Sometimes I am, but I hate to come home to a messy house." He strolled past her, moving Knight to Queen 6, the bed. He tossed back the comforter and patted the mattress. "Even has clean sheets on there for a good night's sleep when I got home."

With an eyebrow raised, Jo cocked her head. "A bed big enough for two with clean bedding. I wanna see that." She walked over, imitating his stroll.

He suppressed a laugh. She was odd, but fun.

She spun around in front of him, sitting on the bed in a smooth rolling motion. Locked in her sickbed her entire life? The girl still had impressive dance moves. She leaned back, running her hands over the sheets. "Nice, but not the satin I expected from such a lady's man."

Brett chuckled, sitting next to her. "You ever tried to 'sleep' on satin? You slide everywhere."

"Sounds like fun."

"It was. Maybe tomorrow night." He leaned down and caught her in a kiss. She melted into him as he laid her back against the bed.

After a few long, wet kisses, she pulled back. "Tomorrow night?" she asked breathlessly.

"Yeah, we're snowed in."

Jo basked in the post-coital bliss. Brett was a monster in the sack, a gifted, generous monster. Any regrets about hopping into his bed faded fast after the first mind-bending orgasm. She curled against his side, her muscles loose, her brain fuzzed. Her eyelids slowly levered shut as a happy moan escaped her lips.

Brett shifted but didn't move away. She put a steadying hand on his stomach, not wanting to lose his heat or the bliss of his skin.

A low chuckle emanated from him. "I'm not going anywhere," he whispered. "Just adjusting." He shifted again, and a warm blanket settled over the two of them. "That's better. Nice and toasty." Pressing a kiss to her forehead, he snuggled in against her. Brett was a cuddler. Who knew?

Her eyes slid shut again. As sleep crept over her, a random thought popped in her head. She gasped, startled, accidentally squeezing Brett. "Oh, shit."

In an instant, he rose to a sitting position, hovering over her, his expression full of concern. "You okay? What's wrong?" He ran a finger along her jawline. *God, how did women not fall in love with him every second of every day?*

She shook her head, the burn of a hard blush on her cheeks. "It's nothing. I realized I've never slept over at a man's house before."

He leaned back, a wry smile on his lips. "Never?" The word held a level of "I smell bullshit" in it.

Sitting up to face him, she placed a hand on his arm. "Not really. No."

His eyebrows raised, he asked, "You weren't a... um... because you've got exceptional skills and..." He cut the sentence off and rifled his fingers through his hair.

Stifling a giggle, she ran her fingers up and down his bicep. "No, not a virgin. But it's kinda sad at my age that it's my first 'sleepover.' I'm so pathetic." She pulled her hand away, as a silly stupid emotion wrenched her gut.

Grown-ups don't do sleepovers and don't admit when they lack sexual skills to a man they'd slept with repeatedly within a short time frame. God, she felt like a hussy, a glutton, but who could resist him?

Guilt ate at her, and the desire to run and lock herself in the bathroom stole over her. But Brett could handle any locked door. Her head low, she blinked hard to bite back tears.

"Whoa," Brett whispered, grasping her hand before she escaped. "What's going on here? If you don't want to sleep here, I can..."

She cut him off, hating she might've hurt him. "No, it's... I feel... Ugh, my entire life is an open field now, and I'm a little terrified. And questioning my decisions. Like coming here with you."

"Oh." He withdrew his hand and slid back on the bed. "I can drive you to another hotel, or um..."

Guilt and trepidation washed over Jo. She stuck her foot in it, insulted the man she'd just made love to, spurned his feelings, and his bed. She lunged for his retreating figure, grasping his hand.

"No." Her voice held no demand but no whine either. "It's not you or this. It's great. You're great."

Dammit, gush much? She dialed back.

"I guess I never thought about sleeping in someone else's bed. I never went to a sleepover as a kid and never stayed the night with a man. It's my first time. So embarrassing." She hid her face.

"Huh," he said, rolling into the bed, coming closer, folding her outstretched arm against his body. "A virgin after all." He crushed her into a kiss, and the bliss bloomed again. How could she doubt anything around Brett?

Chapter Eighteen

Jo woke to a loud trill. She sat up in bed, blinking hard. A pitch-black room surrounded her. Attempting to catch her shaky breath, she grasped for something to cover her naked body. A man's voice sounded off in the distance, and everything sunk home in her tired brain.

Brett's house.

Brett's room.

Brett's naked body.

With a grin, she popped a toe out of bed, ready to search for him.

The blistering cold of his hardwood floor stopped her. With a hiss, she drew her foot under the cover and buried herself. The old woodstove wasn't sending up much heat. She shivered.

Footsteps sounded where she assumed the door was. Damn, it was dark. With no moon and no lights...

Brett called out. "Hey, it's me. It's the landline phone. I'm old-fashioned." He chuckled. "Your mom found us, and she wants to speak to you. Care to come over to my ancient phone and talk to her?"

Jo snuggled deeper into the covers. "Can't you bring me a handset?" She put a ton of pout in her tone.

"No. No power, so it doesn't work." He paused. "I think you need to talk her down." His words were soft, filled with kindness. Most men wouldn't have been so sweet when a date's crazy mother called their house. Never mind, the two of them were well over the legal age of consent.

With a sigh, she pulled off the covers and shivered. "Got a robe or something?"

"Oh, yeah. Don't move." The creak of his tread on the hardwood slid to the left and back to the bed. Her eyes adjusted enough to see his outline as he closed in on her. She took the offered robe, sadly noticing he wore a t-shirt and sweats.

So much for Naked Brett.

The robe on her shoulders, she padded after him, her bare feet sounding too loud in the quiet house. In the kitchen, the kerosene lantern burned brightly, blinding her. Brett noticed and turned the light down a bit. He pointed to the wall between the hall and dining room.

In the center of the small wall sat a red rotary phone. Unable to help herself, she laughed aloud, pointing at the ancient thing. "What the hell is that?"

Brett smirked. "Funny story. It came with the house. The old guy I bought the place from rented it from AT&T for decades. I called 'em and bought that baby outright. She's all mine now." He stepped over and grabbed the receiver, lying upside-down on top of the base. "Your mother." He wandered to the table and sat down.

Tentatively, she picked up the handset. "Hello?"

"It's about time." Her mother's voice sounded shrill and angry. "How long does it take to answer a phone? You didn't answer your cell, nor did that Kramer man. What is going on, Josephine?"

The phone to her chest, Jo pulled in a long breath, her gaze fixed on the ceiling. She could do this. Besides, Mom tried to screw her over with a wedding. Time to take something back.

"You see, Mom." She kept the sarcasm to a minimum, but some leaked through. "There's a snowstorm, and the power is out. My phone is dead. I'm only speaking with you because Brett has an actual landline phone. What do you want?"

She slapped her forehead. Wrong question, and an invitation for Mom to drone on about her needs, Jo's disappointing behavior, and the embarrassment the whole thing caused. Jo waited, but no response came.

"Mom?"

"Are you safe?" she asked, her voice low and tense. "We figured out you ran off with that brute, and I worried for your safety. You shouldn't be..."

Jo cut her off. "I'm fine, Mom. Brett is a gentleman."

"Well, he didn't seem like one when I found him in your room sans clothing. Really, Josephine..."

After years of her mother's overprotective bullshit, Jo cut to the chase. "I'm fine. Do you want to talk about the elephant in the room?"

"What do you mean? The man practically kidnapped you, and I was worried beyond belief. I didn't know if you were safe, and with this snow..."

"Mom." Cutting her off was becoming a habit. "It's fine." Jo's teeth clenched so hard her jaw ached. She wanted to have it out with the woman, but over the phone wouldn't be satisfying enough. Jo needed to see her mother's face when she received the dressing down. "Is that all?"

Mom pulled in a sharp breath, her signal for dissatisfaction. She never raised her voice, but she ripped people apart with a sharp words spoken in a mellow tone.

"No, it's not all, young lady. Come back and apologize to these people for the chaos you caused. You walked out without a word to our guests. Rude on an unbelievable level, Josephine."

Drawing in a breath through her nose, Jo stood tall. Her jaw tight, she said, "You tried to marry me off, Mom. You said a Christmas party, not a sham wedding. I owe you and those guests nothing."

Silence fell on the other side of the line. Jo waited almost a minute before her mother spoke again. "I don't like your tone. We'll discuss it when you arrive." Mom hurried on before Jo broke in again. "The hotel requires that Brett return now. The power is out, and the snow is bad. We only just found this the number to reach him. Put him on the phone."

Jo shook her head. "You're in charge of building maintenance?"

Mom sighed. "Of course not, Josephine." Man, she threw Jo's full name around tonight. "The manager wishes to speak with him."

She held the receiver out to Brett. "Stanley wants a word with you. There are issues at the hotel."

Brett rolled his eyes but took the phone. He pressed a hand over the mouthpiece. "You're aware they hired me as a carpenter for renovations, right?" He winked.

"Apparently, they aren't." She shrugged and whirled into a chair at the table, lamenting the lack of power meant no coffee.

"Yeah?" he asked into the receiver.

"Save my ass," Stanley said on the other end of the line.

With a chuckle, Brett delivered a mock whisper. "Well, big-boy, I didn't know you felt that way."

"Shit, Brett." Stanley's voice held some anguish. "I have a hotel full of pissed-off people, the power is wonky, and a bunch want to leave. I don't have the staff to clear the entrance or the parking lot."

Brett quirked his eyebrows. The place should have a system for snow, being in Upstate and close to a dozen ski places. He sat at the table near Jo, grasping her knee, giving it a little caress. "No one should drive in this mess. Much less those snooty Downstaters. Do they know how to navigate in the snow?"

Stanley cleared his throat. "Look, you gotta fix the power." His voice became muffled, as if he were hiding his words from Jo's mother. "Your girl's ma is out of control. She's made the crazy even crazier. Come back, repair the generators, and clear the lot. I'll pay big time."

Brett grinned. "Oh, yes. You will."

"I called your brothers, too. Ted is out, but Ryan's already on his way. God bless you rednecks with your four-wheel-drive trucks."

Anger coiled in his gut. Forget the redneck comment, which normally would have earned Stanley a beatdown. But he called Ryan? Seriously? Why did Little Brother have to be called in?

Dealing with Jo's mother sucked bad enough, but to add stuck-up, know-it-all little bro to the mix? He didn't need this shit. For one full second, he considered refusing the job, throwing Jo over his shoulder, and staying in bed until spring.

Jaw tight, he said, "Ryan, huh? Before you called me, you called him?"

On the other end of the phone, Stanley hedged with an odd sound in his throat. "Well, I called your cell, then the shop. Your dad always used to be there, day or night. I got Ryan. The call must have forwarded, and..."

His words became faster and faster as Brett's silence loomed. Finally, the guy lost his cool.

"Jesus, Brett. I thought we were doing this legit, with the right forms and paperwork filed. Not on the DL behind Ryan's back. I mean your dad."

Rage burst up from his stomach. No longer a little tickle in his gut. Ryan, always Ryan. Brett, Dad, and Ted made Kramer and Sons what it was. Ryan breezed into town and everyone peed their pants to get ahold of him. Ryan was no better at carpentry and electric than another Kramer. Why did they fawn over him when Brett stood there, tools in hand, ready to get the job done?

Time to stop the nonsense. "Shut up, Stanley. I'll be there when I can. Tell Ryan." Standing, he crossed to the phone base and slammed the receiver down. He kept the old red phone for the satisfaction of doing that. Clicking *End* on a cell phone didn't feel the same.

A light touch danced on his arm, and he spun, ready to launch his fury. Jo stood next to him, her eyes wide.

Brett stepped back. "I'm sorry, Jo. I just..." He scrambled for the right words. "Stanley called my little brother, and..."

"And it pushes your buttons?" she asked. "You mentioned things were tense, but I didn't realize it was that bad. What's the deal?"

Brett scrubbed the back of his neck, feeling stupid and childish for the rivalry. But it still chapped his ass whenever Ryan bested him. Not supposed to be in charge of the company, not supposed to have the best job, best girl, best everything. Ted first, then Brett, and maybe something left over for the little shit.

"I, uh..." He didn't know where to start. "Ryan took over my dad's business, kinda shutting out me and my other brother. I work for him now."

"And you hate it?" She raised an eyebrow, but not her voice, as if she weren't judging him.

Curious.

"Of course, I hate it. He's my little brother. I don't want him to be the boss, my boss. I've worked for Dad since I was sixteen. He never considered me when he handed over the company to Ryan. Now I'm stuck."

A nervous tickle danced along his limbs. It always happened when he focused too much on perfect Ryan and his complete success in the universe. Brett threw up his hands and headed for the mudroom.

"Now I gotta go dig out the Excelsior, and Ry is probably already there, finished the work, and fixed the rest of the old wing." He huffed, pulling on his coat, knowing half of what he said constituted bullshit, and the other half made him feel like a failure.

"Huh," Jo said. She studied him from the kitchen as he threw on his big coat. "But you are going to the hotel anyway?"

He glanced over in time to see her raise an eyebrow, and he scoffed. "I gotta go. It's my job. You can stay here. I'll ramp up the woodstove, and the couch is comfy." He sat on the bench to pull his boots on, and Jo slid in next to him.

"You'll need some help."

"No. And your mother..."

"It's my problem. Let me help. I can talk to your brother." She nudged his shoulder.

"My brother is my problem. Look, I'm gonna head back, plow the parking lot, and shovel some. Fix the generator." He shrugged.

"Let me help with the snow and the brother. Well, at least I can be there for you." She cocked her head, looking like an adorable puppy. Why the hell she did she want to insert herself into his stupid problems? 'Course, he'd never once mentioned problems at work with any woman he dated. Were he and Jo dating? He did sleep with her on her wedding night. The thought drew a smile to his lips, and he let out a chuckle.

"Fine. Come with. But Ry's got a new chick. So don't even think about..."

"Running off with your brother after dallying with you?" She rolled her eyes to the ceiling as if considering.

Brett nudged her this time.

She met his gaze, a wry smile on her lips. "I would never. Besides, it's a matter of perspective. Like with my mother. She's always seen things one way. And I saw it differently. You and Ryan need to check your point of view." She tapped his arm and stood. "Which one of these giant coats won't swallow me whole?"

Chapter Nineteen

Jo sat quietly in Brett's truck as they pulled into the Excelsior's lot. The trip had taken a while. He epitomized the perfect winter driver. Every drift, every deep pile, every awkward stop became child's play for Brett. He even stopped once to help someone out of a jam. She liked him a little more with each mile back to the hotel.

Not to mention, his superior driving distracted her from thinking about her mother and the confrontation awaiting her. Worry wasn't the adjective to describe her mindset. More disinterested amusement. Mom could say whatever she wished. Jo had no use for anything she might say at this point. *A surprise wedding, who does that?*

She was here for Brett. Her whole purpose in returning stemmed from his expression when talking about his brother. With no siblings, she didn't understand the rivalry, but Brett felt it—and hard.

She wanted to support him, but also show that people in their thirties don't need those birth-order roles anymore. He was a man in his own right, but a reminder never hurt.

The exterior of the Excelsior looked both menacing and inviting when they pulled up. Piles of white fluff covered every surface. How would he plow out the white lumpy blanket of a parking lot? The snow made the place seem homey, but the rows of dark windows lent an ominous atmosphere.

No lights shone in the lot, and a few rooms were lit on the left side of the building, where her room and most of the wedding guests were. Odd flickers flashed on the first floor, and one window shone brighter than daylight. *What is going on?*

Brett hemmed as he drove through the lot. He'd already lowered the plow on his truck and moved through the strip to the end of the last row. He turned and headed down the first row, but it was already plowed. The semi-clear asphalt path ended at another pickup parked by the front door.

Brett sighed.

"Ryan's here already. Doesn't it figure? He must have jumped in his truck as soon as the call went out. Son of a bitch." Brett slammed a fist on the dash, his jaw tight.

Jo placed a hand on his arm, urging him to ease up the white-knuckled grip on the steering wheel. "Does it matter? He's plowed one row, and the power isn't fixed yet. You still have time to swoop in and rescue everyone."

He scoffed. "I'm no superhero," he said, slumping in his seat. Deftly, he plowed out several parking spaces and backed the truck into one.

Jo grinned. "Who says you're not?" She placed a chaste kiss on his cheek. "Now let's go save the day." She rubbed her hands together, a smile crossing her lips.

"Yeah, but your ma... I don't want you to think you have to..." He hesitated. *How cute.*

Turning to face him, she said, "Brett. I'm an adult. I can handle my mother. I'm not at fault here." She stated the words with cool confidence, hoping he'd see the similarity in his situation. She knew nothing about the real dynamic between the man and his brother. There might be some serious underlying conflicts. If she could face her mother, he'd deal with Ryan.

He stared at her for a moment, then blinked as if coming out of a trance. "Okay. First, we'll talk with Stanley and get a job list. I'll divide up the work with Ryan. I don't know if Stanley's day guy is still here or not. But since he couldn't fix the Wi-Fi, I got no hope he'll get the generator running." He pulled in a deep breath and exited the truck.

Brett closed the door with a bit of slam. The anger still boiled in his stomach, but Jo made an excellent point. They were adults. Ryan had no right to call him down like a little kid. He'd help Stanley and put the place back on its feet. Just another snowstorm, the same as the eight last winter. He crossed to the back of the truck in time to meet Jo walking around from her side. He put his hand out for hers as if they'd done it a million times.

Head ducked, she gripped his hand, her cheeks pink. Probably from the wind. But he grinned anyway, loving her shyness. Together, they strode inside. The lights in the lobby flickered, dimmed, and then brightened in the three seconds they stood there. The clerk, Tiffany, stood at the desk. Her mouth opened in an O when she saw Jo's hand clasped in his. *Good, maybe now the chick will leave him alone.*

"Where...?" he started, but Tiffany raised her arm and pointed to Stanley's office. Brett nodded and pulled Jo in after him. No way was he leaving her without backup. Tiffany probably already grabbed the phone to dial up Jo's ma.

Inside Stanley's office, the tension was palpable. Ryan stood on one side of the desk, Stanley on the other. Their matching scowls spoke volumes. Brett's gaze flicked from one man to the other, Jo's words echoing in his ears. "See him as another adult."

"What's the 'sitch?" he asked, ready for Ryan to berate him for arriving late or leaving, or for Stanley to complain about the quality of his work. Neither man said a word, just stood scowling at each other. He glanced back and forth between the two, waiting for an answer.

None came.

I don't need this shit.

"What's the biggest issue? Power or a snow-plower?" He grinned at his little joke. Jo slapped his arm, and he winked at her. She shook her head.

"Apparently, the building has many power issues, starting with the Wi-Fi today," Ryan said. "Know anything about that?" His gaze swiveled to Brett, but the anger still pointed straight at Stanley.

What the fuck?

"Yeah, Jo and I fixed..." Brett glanced at the lovely Josephine. "Jo fixed it. The router had... issues, and she handled it. So what's the problem now?"

Ryan opened his mouth to speak, but Stanley cut him off. "The power situation is more complicated than the Wi-Fi thing." He waved a hand as if dismissing the issue. "Ernie failed to inform me about the problems with the panels downstairs.

He also neglected to do maintenance on our backup generators. We are in a hole here, gentlemen." He glared at Ryan, and something prickled at Brett's neck.

"Don't fucking tell me you are blaming Kramer and Sons for your current situation." Brett scowled at the manager. "The hotel is a big fucking place, and you should have a dozen guys working here to keep it up."

Stanley held up a hand to speak, but Brett plowed through him.

"You hired us to renovate a few old rooms, not to do electrical work, not to plow your lot, not to maintain your generators."

"Perhaps you don't understand the entire situation here, Brett." Stanley's tone implied Brett was a toad of a blue-collar worker.

Brett snorted through his nose at the comment. *Fuck him.*

Ryan placed a hand on Brett's arm. He snatched it away, turning his fury on his little brother.

"Did you or Dad forget to mention something when you sent me here?" He filled the words with anger and sarcasm, not caring if it cost him everything—the job, the girl, the brother.

Ryan blinked at him. As usual, he seemed clueless when he fucked up and someone called him on it.

"Whoa, Brett. Let's put the blame where it lies. Stanley called me when the power went out, and he didn't understand how to get the generators running."

The tension built higher until the air seemed too thin to breathe. *I should leave.* He wanted to take Jo home and enjoy a nice quiet snowy weekend with her. Not sit here and listen to more bullshit about his terrible job skills.

He reared back, ready to blast both men for their assholeness and rage-quit, but Jo grabbed his hand. "Hold on there, superhero. What is the conflict here, gentlemen? Was Brett hired as a contractor, or a maintenance man?"

Damn, she put it so precisely, he could kiss her. But better not. It might blow his angry mindset, and these two might need a beat down.

"Contractor," Ryan said.

"Maintenance," Stanley said.

Ryan scratched his chin and glanced over to Brett. "What's your call, bro?" A twinkle in his eye said he was up to something.

Brett stared at his little brother for a second before it clicked. He pulled out his phone and scrolled through the documents on there. Dad always insisted they have the paperwork for every job with them. Digitizing the records had been Brett's idea.

He tapped the doc on his phone. "Here's the contract from the owners, signed for the job—Spencer Drake and Oliver Weston." He handed the phone to Stanley. "It says here: Renovation to west wing's bathrooms. Seems clear to me, but we can call Mr. Drake or Mr. Weston for clarification."

Stanley threw his hands up. They had beaten him. Stan was always a schemer. Nice to watch the old con artist taken down a peg.

"So, when we're done plowing, I expect a check to be ready." He winked at Ryan and led Jo out into the lobby.

Chapter Twenty

Brett stamped the snow off his boots before entering the Excelsior again. The wonder twins stood at the desk, eyeing him with disdain. Who cared? He did the job, saved Stanley's ass again.

The now-functioning generator slowly heated the frosty hotel. The parking lot was clear, and he managed not to bury any guest cars as he cleaned. Job done, mostly by himself. After shoveling the sidewalks, Ryan must have scuttled back to Stanley's office to drink the good scotch.

Fuck them anyway. Brett solved the problem on his own, as he'd done a thousand times for Dad.

Inside the building, he made for the lounge to find Jo. Hopefully, her monster of a mother wasn't aware she'd returned. He pictured finding her as he did the first day, nose buried in her laptop, oblivious to the universe around her. He'd have to break her of the habit. Not because he wanted all her attention, but some blue-collar boob might proposition a pretty woman on her own and end up taking her home. Thank God, he was the first idiot to hit on her.

Before he disappeared into the lounge, the office door opened. Ryan called to him.

Yep, drinking the scotch with the asshole. Brett grumbled.

"Can I speak to you a minute?" Ryan asked.

Brett stopped short with a huff. He was tired, smelly, and wanted to take his new girl home. He had no desire to fight with him.

"Sure," he said, without too much disgust. He spun around and marched into the office, not bothering to glance at his brother.

Throwing himself into the armchair, Brett scowled, poised to defend himself and quit the job. Not the best decision, but he wasn't ready to lose face with Ryan yet.

No Stanley behind the desk. What the...? He glanced over at Ryan, who plunked down in the chair next to him.

"Fifteen minutes to get the generator going again?" Ryan spoke the words with a casual air, which made the hair on Brett's neck stand on end. His brother let out a low whistle. "Impressive."

Brett glowered. "I had to dig the damned thing out. Snow and ice covered the intake because Stanley can't hire a competent maintenance man." He crossed his arms over his chest, waiting for the other shoe to drop. No way Ryan would be nice after that.

"Stanley and I were talking. He thinks he found the perfect maintenance person." He tipped his head, and Brett received the message loud and clear.

Maintenance at an old hotel? Fixing Wi-Fi, cleaning clogged drains, and rewiring ancient outlets. Yeah, the dream job he always wanted—cleaning other people's shit for a living.

Great.

Since he no longer wanted to work for Kramer and Sons, he might not have a choice. The commute would suck, but maybe Stanley could swing rooms for him to live in.

He blinked, not wanting to consider that road yet. He wasn't ready. He wanted to spend a snowstorm stuck with his new lady, listening to her crazy computer stories, and enjoying her body. Ryan's gaze never faltered for a second.

Brett sighed. Time to embrace the inevitable. "So, where's Stanley with a cherry offer for me? I don't got all night." He pressed his lips together, regretting the words as soon as they left his mouth.

Ryan blinked, sitting back in his chair. "He and I... talked. He wanted to know what kinda deal to offer to get you here permanently."

"Please tell me you didn't sell me to the bastard for magic beans, Ry. I'm in no mood for this. I spent the last couple hours..."

Ryan held up a hand. "Stanley threw some interesting carrots out there. Salary in the mid-seventies, free room, discount at the restaurant."

Brett threw his hands in the air and bolted from the chair. He paced the room as Ryan sat watching. An offer like that? More than he made at Kramer and Sons. But he'd be working for Stanley, a bigger dick than Ryan. And just maintenance, not building, creating, working with people to make their dream project become a reality.

He didn't want that.

He stopped behind his chair, gripping the top of the headrest. "Where's Stanley with his great offer?" he repeated.

Ryan crossed his legs, his posture pure relaxation. "I asked him for a minute of your time first."

Here came the counteroffer. Family tradition, loyalty, and Dad's wishes as the topping on the cake. He braced his arms, ready to say no to whatever Ryan was about to offer.

"So... I'm not blaming Dad. You know how he is. Find a problem, fix it. Never considering the human side of things."

Brett said nothing. But his pulse quickened. Invoking Dad so quickly?

Fuck.

"He was mad at Ted," Ryan continued, "about the fire in Stonewater, and how Ted reacted to everything. It turned out we weren't at fault at all. But the damage was done, according to Dad."

Chin raised, Brett narrowed his gaze at his little brother. Again, the idiot hadn't bothered to find out the complete story. "Cheryl dumped Ted hard—left him and disappeared. He hasn't heard from her in a year. Keeps that damned engagement ring in his truck. Never had a chance to give it to her."

Ryan's eyebrows lifted. "Cheryl Winston? He wanted to propose? I didn't know..."

Brett cut him off. "No, you don't know, because you and Dad are so busy solving problems, you forget to actually talk to the humans involved. Like you arranging for my next job while I worked outside. Glad you and Stanley see fit to allow me to work at all."

An ugly well of anger built in his gut. *Fuck this*. He didn't need Ryan's recommendation or Stanley's stupid mediocre job. He had savings, skills, and some reputation to fall back on. City people were always moving to Upstate and wanting to renovate the crap out of old barns, camps, and farmhouses. He'd begin again on his own, maybe with Ted.

His shoulders dropped, and he released his death grip from the top of the chair. Everything seemed so clear.

Start over on his own.

He could do it.

And some cute computer chick could help him set up a website and marketing plan, something Kramer and Sons did not have. He smiled at his little brother as the last of the anger abated.

Ryan cocked his head, glancing sideways at his brother. "Brainstorm there?" He pushed on, not allowing Brett to answer. "Dad was wrong." He met Brett's gaze. "He never should've given me the company without talking to the three of us. It's a family business. We've all done something to make it succeed. You and Ted especially. Ted and I have talked a bit since it happened. He seemed relieved he didn't have to be in charge anymore. He wants more than installing water heaters and making man-caves." Ryan shrugged.

"He's cool with you being the boss?" Brett let his words drip with skepticism. How could Ryan understand what Ted was going through right now? The man was a mess, and his work suffered. But once his broken heart mended, he'd be fine, ready to take charge and kick butt again.

"For now, yes. But unfortunately, you weren't there when it went down. And we haven't talked." Serious blame tainted his words, but Brett merely raised his chin. He was the injured party here. No way he'd apologize.

No fucking way.

"You left me out of the loop. Grabbed your share and mine and Ted's."

Ryan stood, leaving the chairs between them. "It just... happened. You know Dad. I thought it best to let the heat die down. Talk to you and Ted without Dad. I called Stanley about the job here. He said you wanted to stay. Looks like the wires crossed..."

Brett shook his head and stood. No way was he letting Ryan stand over him. "Seriously, you think I wouldn't want to be in on the discussion of a company change?"

Ryan sighed, his chin dipping to his chest. "I followed Dad's lead. I shouldn't have. He should've talked to you, but he didn't." He raised his gaze to meet Brett's. "I was wrong, big bro."

Brett huffed, but a sense of relief filled him. Maybe Ryan wouldn't be such a dick about it after all. The unoffered job from Stanley loomed over them. He didn't want to screw his future. He'd built a good reputation with Kramer and Sons. Unsure how to proceed, he scrubbed his chin. Bills were still due, and independent contracting might not give him the income he needed.

"So, uh," Ryan hedged, rubbing the back of his neck. "You want to work for Stanley? Because honestly, he's kind of a dick."

Brows furrowed, Brett said, "I'll be working for one dick or another. You, him, me." He threw his hands up. "I gotta work."

"Of course. What's your best skill?"

"You giving me a job interview?"

Ryan chuckled. "I manage people and stuff well—organizing things, dealing with customers. I know the codes and more or less how much jobs should cost. But I'm not an expert electrician or carpenter. Ted's amazing with wood, and..."

The last comment forced a guffaw from Brett. "Good with wood? He gonna be the company porn star?"

The joke broke the tension in the room. Ryan slid into the chair, holding his gut. Once he caught his breath, he said, "It's not a direction I thought the company would go. See, Brett? You're the idea man. I need an idea man." He held up a hand. "Though if we do get into porn, Ted might not be the best star. Just putting it out there."

Laughter erupted from his lips, and Brett fell into the other chair. "I don't know. Kramer and Sons' Porn might not work. I'll have to look into the market, the laws in New York, and of course, an actual star for the movies. I might be willing if you give me a decent offer."

Joking with his brother felt good. The two of them used to have similar nonsense conversations when they were kids. They could go for hours, talking about absolutely nothing, and end up with belly aches from laughing so hard.

He grinned at his little brother, more hopeful than he'd been a few minutes ago. Once the laughter settled, Ryan pointed at Brett. "Dad said you came up with everything for the job, spoke with Stanley, and illustrated how to repurpose the old rooms. Had the architect on speed dial and boom, you got a two-month job which made good money for us."

Brett shrugged. No disputing the truth. He'd brokered the deal and made it happened. He did it more often than the rest of his family realized. With a small town and other contractors in Albany and Utica, he used his charm to encourage customers with innovative ideas for renovations and additions.

"Can you do that full time for us? A visionary could move the company forward. I need someone who can work with potential customers to drum up business." He held his hand out toward Brett. "Know anyone like that?"

Brett leaned against the chair, gobsmacked. Is that what Ryan thought? The bastard never said anything before. He narrowed his eyes. Same reason he never spoke to Ryan—stupid male stubbornness. But his little bro offered a job with more than nail-hammering and sheet-rocking? Oh, hell yeah.

He studied Ryan. A serious pain in the ass, but usually genuine, though Dad spoiled him rotten as a kid. And he'd made a good point about Dad. The man turned over the company without a word. He left the baggage to Ryan to deal with. But that sounded exactly like Dad. Find a solution, set it in motion, no discussion, no second thoughts.

Like when Earl fired them. Dad never argued for a second with that douche. Instead, he brought the terminated contract to a notary within the hour. He organized the paperwork, communication, billing, just in case. And hadn't he been right to do so?

"So what are you offering?"

"Well, not a porn ring, if you were still hoping..."

They both chuckled, finally seeing eye to eye.

"I need you, Brett. I can't run the company alone. Ted has no interest in management. And you are the heart of Kramer and Sons. What do you say?"

There it was.

The words he desperately wanted to hear—"I need you, Brett."

Tears stung in Brett's eyes. Ryan wasn't tossing him out. He wanted him in and as more than a grunt worker.

"Well, you had a point about the name..." He paused.

"No porn, man. Come on."

Brett chuckled. "Nah, too much work to get rid of body hair. How about we change the name to Kramer Brothers?"

Ryan's face split into an enormous grin. "Deal!" He rose from his chair, hand out to shake on the deal. Something in Brett's chest quieted. For the first time in his life, he saw a settled future head. Grinning to himself, he shook the offered hand.

Chapter Twenty-One

Jo tapped at her laptop, checking her email again for a reply from the software company. The storm had played havoc with the power, and therefore the Wi-Fi. Even with a hotspot on her phone, she had little access.

She closed the screen. They'd either like her game or not. If the answer from Ezgamez was no, she'd find another job in programming. Between all the online vendors, someone would be glad to have her on their team.

She learned from the debacle with her mother to be independent. No more bowing or scraping. No more letting her gratitude for her mother's help stop her from busting out and living her own life. She might not have much to her name, but she'd live on her own and do the work she loved. Maybe with Brett by her side or not. He was willing to sacrifice it all to be his own man. A perfect example for her to follow.

She eyed the doorway, wondering about Brett and his brother. Keeping him company while he plowed the lot gave her the serious feels for him. They hardly said a word to each other, just enjoyed the quiet silence like some old married couple. Visions of spending time with him sent tingles all over her body. She hoped for more.

Her email notification chimed, and Jo clicked the icon before even realizing it was from Ezgamez. The message was short and sweet. "Welcome to the team! Exceptional game. Final paperwork attached. We'll call on Monday with the official startup stuff."

Jo sighed, relief flooding through her.

New energy in her heart, she gazed at the falling snow outside the lounge window. Life started now. She daydreamed about a life of waking up next to her blond hunk. She sighed. Yeah, she could get used to that. No matter what happened with the brother, she'd tell him how she felt. Tell him she wanted him, even if his stupid brother kicked him to the curb.

The sound of someone clearing their throat brought her gaze to the doorway of the lounge. Mom stood there, dressed in a velour tracksuit. Jo resisted rolling her eyes. *When did Mom get old enough for that outfit?*

She stared hard at her mother, saying nothing. What could she say to a woman who planned a surprise wedding? Mom walked into the room, her chin low but her gaze steady on Jo. Thankfully, Dexter did not follow in her wake.

Jo settled into her chair, tipping the laptop's screen to block her work. Thank God she finally took the plunge and applied for the job.

She lifted her chin, defiant and angry. She'd never hate her mother outright, but the whole planning-her-life-without-her- permission thing—hell, without her knowledge. A bolt of irritation drove up her spine, and she clenched her teeth.

"Josephine." Mom's tone sounded relaxed, indifferent, but behind the word, annoyance loomed. "I heard you returned to the hotel. With that man." Her gaze rolled toward the lounge door. "I didn't think you'd be back."

She ran her hand along the back of the chair opposite. Her eyes never met Jo's. "I called several times. Your safety, my chief concern. There's a snowstorm out there." She waved a hand at the window where the snow continued to rain down.

Unable to help herself, Jo snorted. "You realize Brett is the guy the hotel called to fix their problems? The snow and the electricity?" She shook her head. Mom would never understand. No use to explain he wasn't a predator.

Mom pulled the chair out and took her time sitting down. She ended up perching on the end of the seat as if the thing might bite her if she sat back and relaxed.

Jo repressed another snort.

"I understand my call brought him here. Had you answered your cell phone..."

Jo held up a hand. "Don't play martyr here, Mom. You tricked me. You treated me like a child. And like a child, I ran. But I came back, to help Brett, but also to talk to you. Face to face." She closed the laptop.

Mom opened her mouth, but Jo jumped in before she began.

"You ambushed me."

"You said that." Mom's tone sounded snotty, hurt.

Jo didn't care.

"A wedding, Mother. An entire wedding without so much as a word to me about it. What woman in her right mind would want a surprise wedding? A shower? A birthday party? Yes. But a wedding isn't something you toss at the bride."

Mom crossed her arms. "Jo, let's not quibble here. We both know you require a caretaker." She let her gaze meet Jo's for a split second. "Dexter is fully qualified as a husband. He has money, stability, good health. If the carpenter had an accident, you'd be in a world of trouble."

"Okay. You've missed something. Did you understand what Dr. Miller said? I have celiac."

Mother spun from her chair and marched dramatically to the window. "I know." Her voice spoke of forlorn women, desperate mothers, woe-laden lives. "Why do you think I put the wedding together? Celiac." She clucked her tongue. "A life sentence." She dabbed under her eye with her sleeve.

Jo laughed so hard she fell on the floor.

"Josephine!" Her mother dashed to her side. "My God. Are you all right?"

Through hiccups and guffaws, Jo swatted her mother away.

"Let me help you."

Her tone quelled Jo's laughter. "I'm laughing at you, Mom. Because you are hysterical. A true hypochondriac. Do you understand what celiac is? Did you listen at all? I have to stay away from gluten. That's all."

Mother shook her head. "The doctor dismissed your past with the new diagnosis. It can't be that simple. I tended you through your horrible childhood. You were so sickly, thin. Your bones broke, and you threw up all the time. You wasted away before me." She sobbed, throwing herself into the chair again, her forearm covering her eyes. "How we both suffered."

"Yes, Mom. It was tough. We both struggled because we didn't realize the cause of my sickness. But now we do. And yes, it's that simple. I became malnourished because I can't process wheat. It made me sick. All those crackers, bread, and cookies made it worse."

Mom lay her head down on the table, her sobs palpable. "I did the best I could for you."

Jo rubbed her mother's shoulder. "Yeah, you did. You took great care of me. But now I know what's wrong. I can live with the condition easily."

Mom's head popped up, and she shoved Jo's hand away. "You have a lifelong sentence with this disease. That's why I spoke with Dexter. We agreed your marrying him would provide you with the health care you require."

Mom was still not listening. The drama and whining got them nowhere. Jo buried her anger once again. After a cleansing breath, she stared hard at her mom.

"One, the world is quite aware of gluten allergies now, so my diet will be easy to manage. Two, you and Dexter, who isn't even my boyfriend, don't get to decide what's best for me. I need you as a parent and a friend, but not a caregiver. I can take care of myself."

"You don't need me anymore." Her mother dropped her head back on the table, the sobs louder. "After all I've done for you."

"Jesus, Mom." The core of molten anger in her gut exploded. The years of bowing and scraping only to have to show gratitude to someone who kept her prisoner. *Uh, no.* Mom didn't see and might never. Jo let the anger roar through her and out her mouth.

"I'm an adult, and I deserve an actual life outside your care. It's a manageable allergy. I'm not waiting anymore, Mom. Be happy I'm better. I have a job, met a nice guy, and I'm moving out. You can't stop me."

Anger spent, the warmth of her emotions still played over her skin. She'd never spoken to her mother like that in her lifetime. It was great to unload on her—to tell her the truth she'd wanted to say for so long. They'd been so co-dependent for so many years.

But the chains were broken. Dammit, Jo wouldn't cow or wait for the woman to understand times had changed.

Mom straightened in her chair, her head up but not looking at Jo. No tear tracks marred her makeup. Either it was quality stuff or the crocodile tears failed to leave their mark.

"I don't know how you'll survive. If you're on your own... You understand what it means?"

Jo smirked. "Just say it, Mom."

She'd known from the day of the diagnosis this conversation would happen. She'd planned for it. That's why she'd agreed to the party at the hotel. It gave her time to put her ducks in a row and support herself once her mother dropped the ax. And the woman was swinging.

"Can this Brett support you with the health care you require? The lifestyle you are used to? Can he give you what you need?" She threw her words like darts, and Jo dodged every one.

Crossing her arms, she leaned against the wall. "I've got this."

"Not if I refuse to..."

There it was. The "I'll cut you off" sentence Jo waited for.

"I don't need your money, Mom. I have some in trust from Dad. Not much. But I have a new job, and I'm good at it. I sent a sample project into Ezgamez, and they offered me a fantastic position on their team. Good-bye."

Her computer back in the case, she tossed the bag over her shoulder with enough chutzpah for Mom to receive the message. Jo strolled to the door.

Mother called after. "Position? When did you get a job?"

Jo smiled at her and kicked the lounge door closed behind her.

Jo practically ran into Brett in the lobby, his head tipped down, one hand rifling his hair.

Damn. Maybe the meeting with his brother didn't go well.

She had a cure for that. They never finished the "being trapped in a snowstorm together" adventure. Even though he had a plow and a woodstove.

"Hey," she whispered, lightly touching his arm. "Wanna get out of here?"

His head popped up. A foolish grin spread across his face. "Hey, yourself."

"You must be exhausted after all that work, and..." She waved at the closed office door.

"Actually," Brett said, scooping her up in his arms. "I'm good. You still have the key for the suite?" His grin was infectious. A handsome man standing so close muddled her thoughts.

"Room key?"

"We can celebrate." He narrowed his gaze. "Unless it didn't go well with your mother, and you wanna book." He rubbed a hand along her arm.

Tiny bolts of lightning ran up her skin. Her mind raced to all sorts of naughty places.

"How did you know I spoke to Mom?"

The grin returned. He ran a finger over her forehead. "You get this little crinkle right there"—he poked the spot between her eyes—"when you've had a conversation with her. It's as if you can't figure out what happened." He chuckled.

Jo rubbed the bridge of her nose, smoothing the wrinkles. "Yeah, well, we just..." She waved a hand at the lounge door as her mom stepped into view. Jo stiffened, and Brett put an arm around her.

"I assume," Erica said, her tone snotty, "that you still don't intend to go through with the wedding. After our guests..."

Fire burned in Jo's chest.

He leaned close to her ear. "You don't have to listen to a word from her."

She met his eyes. "She needs to understand, Brett." He kissed her cheek and released her arm. "Mom. You're a snowplow. You shove every obstacle out of my way. But that's not what I need. Stop the over-protective nonsense."

Her mother scoffed. "I kept you safe. And this is how you repay me." She waved a hand at Brett and the fire of anger danced along Jo's skin for a second time.

"I'm repaying your love and kindness by becoming a responsible adult. By growing up, being independent, and finding my own way." She stepped toward her mother, angry that the woman insulted Brett.

"It's time for me to live my own life, Mom. To earn my own money, to clean my own socks. To choose my own partner."

The woman's hand fluttered at her neck as if she wanted to reprimand more.

"I have a job and health benefits. I'll be fine." She grasped Brett's hand. "We are going upstairs to my room to celebrate. Good-night, Mom."

Jo walked by the gaping woman, electing to take the stairs rather than wait at the elevator.

As they passed her, Mom said, "I wanted the best for you, Josephine."

"I know," Jo called as they ducked into the stairwell. "You gave it to me, and I ran with it. Thanks, Ma."

The heavy stair door clanged behind them as she and Brett climbed up.

Brett couldn't help but smile. Jo handled it beautifully, better than he did with Ryan. He had to admire his girl.

His girl.

She was.

He liked her spirit and charm... and other assets. But most of all, he loved how she stood up for herself without tearing down her ma. Nice. He could use a few pointers for dealing with his dad.

Close behind her, he worked hard to keep his hands to himself. He desired nothing more than to smash her up against a wall and ravish her. Well, maybe nuzzle her and make out for a bit. He needed more info about her delicate health. The last thing he wanted to do was hurt her.

She opened the suite door and pounced on him before he had a chance to close it. Her mouth hot against his, keening sounds emanating from her lips, she wrapped her legs around his waist and ground against him. With a supreme effort, he tapped down his male ego and held back.

She ended the torturously feverish kiss with a pop. "What's the matter?" Her eyes searched his face, and he hoped he didn't disappoint her. "Don't you want to?"

"I do." His voice sounded deep and rough, "but the stuff with your ma... She understands you're not some mail-order bride?"

Jo smiled. "Well, if she didn't before, telling her about the game deal should have driven it home." She grinned, wiggling against him, driving him toward a caveman brain.

"Great. But I'm no gold digger, woman. I have my own company to run."

Her mouth dropped open. "Wait, your brother gave you the company?"

Brett shook his head. "Partnership. Kramer Brothers, now. We can find a way to work together. As equals."

She squealed. "That's amazing. We are both so awesome."

Wrapping his hands around her butt, Brett adjusted her position. "And horny. Let's celebrate." He duck-walked over to the bed, careful not to jostle her too much.

"Wait," she said as he lowered her. He could wait. He'd wait forever for his Jo.

"So, uh, you're interested in more than a hookup?"

Brett smiled, restraining an eye roll. "Oh, hell yeah."

"Good. I have the room until tomorrow. Let's get to know each other." She grinned, opening her arms. He fell into the embrace, feeling satisfied for the first time in his life.

The End

Check out these titles by Ginny Frost

The Oakwood Tavern Series

The Bar Scene, Oakwood Tavern 1

Terese Brock manages the Oakwood Tavern with style and grace. Unfortunately, she's trying to avoid her employer's IRS disaster and her own debts. She needs a new job—fast. Terese hopes to land an executive position at the new conference center, the perfect solution to all her money woes.

For months, Drew Drake has admired Terese from afar, but she doesn't know he exists. He's thrilled when his humor and persistence catch her eye. And when she takes him home, he discovers she's everything he expected, and so much more.

Drew fails to mention he's the heir to one of the most successful businesses in town, the force behind the new conference center. Rather than clue her in, he decides to let her get to know the real him. When she walks into her interview, ready to kick ass and take names, her universe shatters.

Behind the desk sits her boy-toy, Drew.

Swindled, Oakwood Tavern 2

For years, Marley Volkov's survival depended on conning people out of their life savings. One look into Alan Reid's pained eyes, with his soiled reputation and heap of financial problems, awakens a new empathy inside her. She renounces grifting forever and not just because every inch of her burns to be with him. But his association with her and her checkered past will drag him further into the gutter. To save herself, to save him, she must walk away. Walk away from the unbridled desire he inspires, from the passion and sympathy that feel like home.

Alan Reid is buried to the neck in money issues. The understanding and compassion he finds in Marley is the exact thing he needs at the completely wrong time. Everything about her makes his blood run hot. She's smart, irresistible, and a criminal. Why is the only person who's ever shown him sympathy have to be a con artist? He can't be with her, but he's compelled to save her from herself.

Stranded, Oakwood Tavern 3

Where the hell is Conrad?

While his business partners back at The Oakwood Tavern think he's on the run for tax evasion, for Conrad Bennett, it's a whole other story. One that includes being stranded on an island in the South Pacific with no cell phone, no money, and no passport.

Good thing he just slept with the only woman on the island with a plane.

Vivian Costa has her own problems. She's on this remote island for a much needed, much overdue, self-imposed exile. But now her one-night stand wants not only a ride off the island, but to find out who has set him up. So much for laying low and hiding out. Vivian knows she should walk away, but there's something about Conrad that won't let her.

It's time to figure out how to rescue each other.

When Hearts Collide, Oakwood Tavern 4, Sandy Bay 5

Planning and organizing the wedding this weekend left Stacey Montgomery little time for fun. She's woefully behind on her Bucket List from the bridal shower. Right now, on the plane to Massachusetts, it's her last chance to cross off number three. Luckily, there's a hottie sitting next to her, and he looks promising. And if her plan succeeds, she might invite him for all the other winter activities on the list.

After working through a criminal IRS audit at his job in Iverton, Eric Holmes could use some rest and relaxation. Usually, bad luck plows him flat like a steamroller, but this time his friend Pete caught the bad juju. With his bestie in a cast from a skiing accident, Eric gladly took Pete's place to tend bar at a destination wedding on the Atlantic coast. Then, he sat next to the most beautiful woman—blonde, curvy, and...

She just asked him to join the mile-high club

Gulp.

But how can he say no?

Stonewater Stories

The Carriage House, Stonewater Stories Book 0.5

Homeless, jobless, and newly single, Cheryl Winston-Bristol finds herself back at her oppressive childhood home. Even at the Carriage House of their estate, she can't escape her overbearing mother and tyrant of a grandfather from making her life miserable. That is until she discovers her high school crush, Ted Kramer, repairing the steps. The dozen years of handyman repairs have molded him into quite a hunk.

Ted working around her house every day? Yes, thank you.

Desperate for the work, Ted Kramer of Kramer and Sons agreed to take the job at the Winston-Bristol's Carriage House. Ted is both excited and terrified since most of their family hates his. Then he discovers Cheryl is home and living in the Carriage House. Working in the same place with the beautiful, classy Cheryl terrifies and excites him. He can handle seeing the charming Cheryl all summer, can't he?

In this prequel to the Stonewater Stories, learn how Ted and Cheryl found each other. To hear their happily ever after, read all of the Stonewater Stories.

Christmas Sparks, Stonewater Stories Book 1

Kindergarten teacher, Margaret Porter, is looking forward to the best Christmas holiday in years. Without her irresponsible ex-husband causing chaos, she and her two children can finally have a fun, peaceful celebration. Everything looks picture perfect until her living room catches fire.

Volunteer firefighter, Ryan Kramer, never knew what hit him when he rescues a reluctant and quick-tempered Margaret from her burning home. But it's more than sympathy for her situation that gets under his skin. Her sassy, no-nonsense attitude bowls him over.

Margaret finds her family rescued by Ryan again and again. Something about him speaks to her soul, and she discovers it hard to resist him. Unlike her careless and manipulative ex-husband, Ryan's nothing but wonderful throughout the entire ordeal.

As Ryan investigates the damage to Margaret's home, he discovers his family's business, Kramer and Sons, worked on the fire-ravaged room. Did shoddy work by his family put a single mom and her two kids out in the cold at Christmas? Can Margaret see beyond his last name and fall for him too?

Christmas Baby, Stonewater Stories Book 3

He'd heard the rumors she was back in town. He had to see for himself.

As Ted Kramer steeled himself to knock on the hotel room door, the last thing he was prepared to see was the woman who shattered him holding a baby. Cheryl Winston-Bristol had been the love of his life. And when she abruptly left town last year after their secret summer romance, it destroyed him. He couldn't eat. Couldn't sleep. Couldn't work. Yet here she is, baby and all. His baby. Merry Christmas to him.

When Cheryl realized she was pregnant, she knew her controlling and manipulative grandfather would never accept a Kramer child into his family. The feud between the Kramers and Winston-Bristols had dragged on for forty years and as long as that cantankerous man was alive, it would continue raging. Except now he's dead, and Cheryl has taken the opportunity to return to Stonewater for the services. She knows she needs to tell her mother—and Ted—about the baby, but she never wanted him to find out about his daughter like this, though.

Maybe, just maybe, baby Harper will be the Christmas gift these families need to move on and find love again.

New Year's Miracle, Stonewater Stories Book 4

This past Christmas, Beverly Winston-Bristol's entire world has flipped on its side. Her beloved father passed away, and her errant daughter, Cheryl, has returned with a new baby, a Baby Kramer at that.

Beverly must heal old wounds for the sake of Baby Harper. If she continues her vendetta against David Kramer and his sons, she'll not only lose Cheryl again but her first grandchild as well. But being near David still hurts. Now that they are grandparents together, can Bev deal with having him back in her life?

On New Year's Eve, Harper's crib collapses. Alone with the baby, Beverly has no choice but to call David to rescue her.

Enjoy this sweet edition to the Stonewater Stories.

The Mortar & Pestle Series
Artist: A Second Chance Romance

Lexi Pintari is stuck in a dead-end cubicle job that is slowly killing her. She tucked away her passion for art when the love of her life ghosted her after college. Witnessing her lack of motivation, Lexi's best friend drags her to an art retreat for much-needed reflection and inspiration. Though knowing her ex-boyfriend is an artist-in-residence there, Lexi agrees to go. Unfortunately, her metal-goth style and enthusiasm for graphic comics clash with the pastel-scarf-wearing, tea-sipping participants, making her ex the least of her problems.

Cole MacDougall is blocked. His rise to the top of the modern art scene is crushed by a missing muse. He is desperate to paint again, but the canvas remains blank. Due to the shortage of patronage revenue, he is forced to put up with the groupie-students. Until he sees a woman standing out like a sore thumb in ripped jeans and a leather jacket. Lexi. Hope blooms that he can renew his passion through her.

About the Author

Ginny Frost is an indie author with three great series. She writes contemporary romance with a sexy, funny kick. In her downtime, she plays clerk at the local library—the perfect job to feed her reading addiction.

She lives in upstate NY with her very own kindhearted ogre, their two brilliant and creative children, and an evil cat named Flash.

Find Ginny Frost online

www.ginnyfrost.com